TRAGEDY TRIUMPH ETERNITY

Ian Goldsmith

ISBN 978-1-956001-67-9 (paperback)
ISBN 978-1-956001-68-6 (eBook)

Library of Congress Control Number: 2021919875

Books may be ordered through Amazon.com; Barnes & Noble.com, or any other bookseller, or by contacting the Publisher.

Publisher Name: Westpoint Print and Media
Publisher Website: www.westpointprintandmedia.com
Author Website: http://www.doctorcurtissmithauthor.com

Printed in the United States of America

DISCLAIMER

Characters, places, and incidents are from the author's imagination, and have no relevance to any person, place, thing, or event in real time. Any similarity thereto is purely coincidental.

All information, content, and/or other material presented in this publication, titled ***Tragedy Triumph Eternity*** is for entertainment purposes only. It is not intended to replace, or substitute any financial, professional, nor any other services. Materials presented are the exclusive property of the author, with the exception of any material commonly used in the Public Domain. The author expressly disclaims any/all liability concerning presentation of material, or effect, on any persons following the information provided in this publication, and claim hold harmless release on any/all such claims.

It is not the intent of the author to plagiarize, or intentionally use any copyrighted materials without permission of the copyright holder.

In no event shall the author, namely ***Ian Goldsmith*** (Pseudonym) or Representative, be liable for any special, direct, indirect, or consequential damages, and/or any damages whatsoever, resulting from information, arising out of, or in connection with the use, or performance of any information appearing in this publication.

In the unlikely event that any copyrighted material inadvertently appears herein, with the exception of verbiage used in part from common, every day expressions, and information appearing in Wikipedia, and the Public Domain that may be presented, the author claims hold harmless release privilege.

NOTE: The material in this book is **NOT Politically Correct** and may be offensive, and not suitable for some audiences.

Neither is it intended to be discriminatory, prejudicial, offensive, or insensitive to any age group, culture, ethnicity, gender, race, or religion.

The goal, intent, and purpose, is to share the fictional life story, in real time, of a male teen-age main character, namely, *Phillip Kingsley*, causing the reader, whether they be teen-ager, adult, or aged elder, to relate to, and recall, *with a grin or belly laugh,* their own formative years.

Assuming that will happen, the goal and intent will have been achieved.

ACKNOWLEDGMENT

Acknowledgment is given to my many friends, co-workers, and colleagues who were instrumental, and encouraging in being both counselor and critic, in the pursuit of my attempt to become an author.

To those who have read the manuscript, and have offered suggestions, I am especially indebted.

Appreciation is extended to **Steve Dunn**, for his expertise in designing the front and back covers which is symbolically appropriate to introduce the content.

A Special *"Thank You"* to **Gloria Dunn,** for taking time away from her busy schedule to assist with editing.

To escape embarrassment of omitting someone's name, by mentioning some, and not others, listing of the majority of names has been avoided.

To those who have shared in this experience, know who they are; I am touched and grateful.

Thank you, and God's Blessings

§§§§§§§§§§§§§§§§§§§§

DEDICATION

Ellen Grace Manning

I dedicate this first novel to the memory of my Mother, **_Ellen Grace Manning,_** (deceased), whose faith, love, and sacrifice upheld me through my formative years, with love, gentleness, inspiration, strength, and exceeding patience.

Sgt. Carl A. Smith

I also dedicate this work to the memory of my Brother **_Sgt. Carl A. Smith_**, (deceased), a U.S. Army Veteran WWII, who served with Distinction, and Honor.

When the war ended, he was discharged, and one year later, lost his life in a fatal automobile accident caused by a drunk driver.

§§§§§§§§§§§§§§§§§§§§

PREFACE

The Title: **TRAGEDY TRIUMPH ETERNITY**, describes, and symbolically portray the events surrounding the life of the main teenage character; *Phillip Kingsley.*

TRAGEDY = Death of a Parent; the Father
TRIUMPH = A Spiritual Awakening Transformation
ETERNITY = Life after Death; Eternal Life

This novel was written in the mid 1950's, before the Korean War armed conflict, and was never published. No attempt has been made by the author to plagiarize any copyrighted material.

Fictitious cities, places, events, blue language, slang terms, juvenile slang words, and swear words appear, that were commonly used by teenagers during that particular time frame. All character names are fictitious. To keep the story line consistent with language and terms used during that time frame, some examples are listed below.

1. Public Phone Booth – Now Replaced by Mobile Cell Phones
2. Record Player – Now Replaced by CD player
3. Long Play Records – Now Replaced by Discs
4. Boom Box – Now Replaced by a portable CD player
5. Caddy = Cadillac car
6. Merc = Mercury car

7. Mill = Souped up Vehicle Engine
8. To Wax = To win
9. Second = Second Gear in Manual Transmission
10. Blast = A Good Party Time
11. Hot Roddin' = Riding in a Souped Up Car
12. Joy-Ridin' = Riding Around for Pleasure
13. Cruising the Gut = Slowly Driving Up / Down the Main City Street
14. Draggin' = Drag racing pitting one car, against another car
15. The novel contains strong language, intimate sex scenes, and death occurrences, and may not be suitable for some audiences.

§§§§§§§§§§§§§§§§§§§§§

INTRODUCTION

The shrill cries of excited teenagers shattered the stillness of a peaceful summer day.

"Hit him again! Him again!" Screamed a chorus of voices. Attention was focused on two junior high males engaged in a bloody fist fight. While the onlookers yelled for action, one of the youths ducked a blow, and attempted to run from the fight. The would-be victim was immediately in pursuit. The clamorous crowd of bystanders prevented his escape.

A hush settled over the crowd, when rays from the sun reflected off the shiny steel of a switchblade knife, in the hand of the perpetrator. The victim gave ground, backing away as the assailant brandished the blade in a threatening way. Suddenly, changing his mind, the assailant closed, and pocketed the switchblade. Glancing from left to right, finding an opening, he burst through the crowd, and ran from the fight. Though he had gained momentary advantage, he showed no desire to use the blade. Instead, he fled across the school yard, losing the respect of classmates who, in his defeat, called out to shame him, "Chicken! Coward! Yellow belly!"

§§§§§§§§§§§§§§§§§§§§§

CONTENTS

CHAPTER 1

A Vote of Confidence

Philip Kingsley was an industrious lad, even while in elementary school. He earned spending money by delivering papers, raking leaves, and cutting neighbor's lawns. Big for his age, coupled with a childhood illness he had outgrown, he got a late start in school.

Because he was bigger than most classmates, he felt self-conscious, believing other kids were laughing at him, due to his age and size. This was one of many reasons he lived as he did; quiet, dominant, and serious. These characteristics formed a personality difficult to ignore, and caused classmates to look up to him with respect, and fear. His above average size had saved him from the immediate danger of the switchblade.

Bruce Miller, acting President of the "Dare Devil Club," called the meeting to order. Raucous chatter silenced; the meeting was under way. All eyes turned to Bruce as he spoke. "Guys, since our President Mike English moved away, we need to elect a new President. I'm not interested, so we need to nominate potential candidates. I declare nominations are now open."

Silence prevailed as wits collected and nominations began. Karl Drake rose and nominated Jeff Contessa. Dan Lane nominated Phil Kingsley. Vernon Grayson moved nominations cease. The motion was carried unanimously. Both candidates were asked to leave the room while ballots were cast. James Dudley and Vincent Spears counted the ballots.

The vote was a tie; six for Phil and six for Jeff. Bruce had not voted. Again, all eyes turned to Bruce. Before bringing the candidates back into the room, Bruce paused and spoke.

"Because I like both Phil and Jeff very much, I would really find it hard to know which one to vote for except for the good showing Phil gave us yesterday in the school yard fight. I liked the way he stood up to Duke Fiske, even when Duke pulled the blade. So, for my money, I cast my vote for Phil; he's our new President." Loud applause filled the room as the candidates were brought back into the clubhouse room.

Bruce introduced Phil. "Folks, meet our new President Philip Kingsley."

Another round of applause. Then someone used the old cliché demanding, "Speech! Speech!"

Proud and filled with pride, Phil strode to the front of the clubhouse. He turned, paused, and begin to speak. "I appreciate your confidence to elect me as your President and I am very thankful. I only hope I can do as good a job as Mike did. We had a lot of good times together because of his leadership and planning. I will now ask for any old business." There was no response. "Is there any new business?" After a momentary silence Karl Drake spoke.

"Yeah, man, what are we gonna' do for Halloween? It's only a little more than a week away?"

"Yeah, man. We gotta' think up somethin' real good!" Dan Lane exclaimed.

"Well, how about somebody makin' some suggestions." Phil said.

"I got a real good one, man," Ron Contessa said. "Remember how old man Thompson always yells and cusses us out every time we take a shortcut in walking across his place when we go to school? Let's put his cow on top of his barn!" Ron continued.

"Yeah, man! That's a good one; let's do it!" Vern Grayson quickly consented, little aware of just how the trick or treat would be accomplished.

"All in favor of putting old man Thompson's cow on top of his barn stand up!" Phil said.

All fifteen members of the club jumped to their feet.

"It's unanimous then; we'll do it," Phil said.

"Let's get even with that battle-axe old lady Moore for sicing her dog on us when we climbed over her fence. Let's move her outhouse behind the hole," Vince Spears suggested.

"That's perfect. She deserves it," Bruce agreed. "All in favor of movin' old lady Moore's outhouse behind the hole say 'Aye'." A raucous exclamation of ayes rocked the room. "All opposed say 'nay!'" Silence filled the room.

And so it went, suggestions for prankish revenge, practical jokes and rude acts of mischief were made until suddenly, Phil looked at his watch. "Somebody make a motion to adjourn. I gotta' get home and milk the cow before my old man tans my hide," he explained. A motion was made and seconded; the meeting was adjourned.

Phil reluctantly walked toward home, realizing he had stayed too long at the club. He knew what to expect when he arrived.

CHAPTER 2

Flirting with Temptation

When Phil walked into the yard his dog, Lucky, raced to meet him, barking excitedly. He knelt to greet him, scratched him on the head, and rolled him over to scratch his stomach. Before he reached the door of his house, he could hear the alcoholic rage of his father's boisterous voice. Entering the kitchen his father's wrath launched out at him.

"Where the hell have you been?" he demanded.

"I was with some of the guys after school," Phil explained.

Don't you have enough sense to come home on time, to help your mother, brother, and sister with the chores?" he questioned demanding an answer. Even before Phil could answer his father continued to bark orders to him. "Get out there and milk that cow before I beat the hell out of you."

Phil went to the screened-in porch, picked up the milking pail and stool; with anger at his father smoldering, he headed for the barn. Ever since Phil could remember it had been like this; his father's drinking and "roughing up" the family. It seemed like the older he got, the worse the relationship with his father had become. His mind raced with the thought of how he could hardly wait until he was old enough, to leave home and escape from it all. He only felt sorry for his mother, who every day had to bear the brunt of his father's anger, and meanness.

Walking home from school the next day, his eyes hungrily followed the graceful lines of a big, beautiful car that had just passed. He lived for the day when he could become successful enough to own a car, like he had just seen, to show off to the community, his family, and to himself. That in spite of their belief, he could become "somebody."

The blasting of a horn behind him rudely awakened Phil from his day dreaming. The car rolled by, and slid to a screeching halt. A lithe, graceful young man jumped out. The driver was David Fisher, a school acquaintance of Phil's.

"What's up, man?" he asked. "Not much, Dave; how's things with you?"

"Crazy man! Crazy!" he replied. "What ya' doin' tonight?"

"Nothing, I guess. The old man won't let me use the car until I'm sixteen, and get my license. So, I guess I'll just be stayin' home," he replied.

"Hey man, we're havin' a little party at my folks place tonight. It bein' Friday and all. The old man and old lady are up at our mountain cabin for the weekend. We're gonna' have a blast; wanna' come?" Dave asked.

"You know I would, Dave, but I don't see how I can. My old man keeps a tight rein on me," he replied.

"Aw, don't worry. Climb in. I'll arrange everything with your old man," he confidently said.

"What are you gonna' tell him?" Phil asked.

"I'll tell him you're gonna' spend the night with me, and I'm gonna' help you study up for the drivin' test, so you can get your driver's license when you turn sixteen," Dave said.

"Hey! That might work," Phil replied.

"Sure, it'll work, man. Just leave everything to your 'old Daddy-O,'" Dave jokingly said, with an air of confidence.

As luck would have it, Phil's father was in a really good mood for once. It appeared he had not had enough to drink to become mean and ugly, but just enough to be "feelin' good." As the guys pulled into Phil's drive his dad was coming out of the house. Recognizing Dave's car, he strode over to say hello. Dave and Phil's dads were good friends, and drinking buddies. "Howdy Dave, how are ya?" Verle Kingsley asked.

"I'm good Mr. Kingsley, and yourself?" Dave asked.

"Dandy. Just dandy," Verle replied, and continued, "How's your Pa? I haven't talked to him in a while?"

"He's good also. I'll tell him you asked about him." Dave replied.

"Do that; tell him to call me when it's convenient," Verle requested.

"Say Mr. Kingsley, how about lettin' Dave spend the night at my place for a sleepover. I think I might be able to help him study up for the driver's test." Dave explained.

"That's a good idea Dave. I'm glad I thought of it," he jested with a laugh. Turning to Phil he said, "You'll have to do the chores before you go though."

"Thanks a lot, Mr. Kingsley," he said, slyly winking at Phil. And said, "I'll pick you up about seven."

"You're welcome. Tell your pa hello for me," Verle yelled, as Dave backed out of the driveway.

Phil was overjoyed beyond words. He had been to Dave's parties before, and he fondly remembered with pleasure the good times he had enjoyed.

A few minutes before seven o'clock, Dave pulled into Phil's drive and sounded the horn. Phil waved, and walked toward the car. He hoped his father was dozing on the sofa. Phil didn't want his dad to see the shadows of female images, belonging to other occupants in the car.

"Come on, man; get with it," Dave said. An attractive blonde sat on the seat beside Dave.

Phil opened the car door. Dave introduced Phil to the blonde in the front seat, "Phil, this is Pat Lane; Pat, this is Philip Kingsley."

Phil said, "My pleasure," but was already looking past Pat, to a very lovely, sweetheart faced brunette sitting in the back seat.

Pat turned and introduced them. "Phil, meet my best friend, Eileen Marshall. Eileen, this is Phil Kingsley."

Eileen murmured a husky "Hi."

In an uneven voice Phil said, "It's my pleasure to meet you."

Dave backed the car from the driveway and sped toward his home.

At a loss for words, Phil pulled out a pack of smokes, and offered one to Eileen. At first, she refused by shaking her head, then, changing her mind said, "Oh, alright, I'll have one." There was a slight tremor in Phil's hand when he held a light for her. His face was ashen in the dim glow of the lighter. In his mind, he told himself, he had never met anyone as attractive.

Approaching their destination, the car slowed, and entered a long drive. The Fisher home set well off the highway. The large two-story home, with colonial facade architecture, stood majestically in the silvery moonlight.

Several cars were parked among the trees bordering the house. In the reflection of Dave's headlights, shadows of couples embracing could be seen, "warming up," for activities of the evening, as evidenced by steamed-up windows. Couples came apart when the headlights' brightness pierced the night's darkness.

Stopping the car, Dave jumped out, opened the door for Pat and exclaimed, "Well, here we are folks. Let's roll back the rug, and let the party get underway; everyone will have some fun at Dave's party tonight."

Cases of beer came out of cars, and were carried into the party room, located in the basement of the home. One of the guys had brought along his boom box to provide music for dancing. When everyone arrived the owner of the boom box loaded a disc. A toast was offered by Dave, "to a helluva good time." Music filled the room; the party was in full swing.

Beer flowed fast, and free. Even though 100 proof alcohol, so-called "white lightning" moonshine was available at Dave's father's bar, the guys and gals preferred beer to the rough, raw taste of the "white lightning.'"

Only, and if, beer ran out, as a last resort, would they attempt to drink the moonshine to obtain the desired effect of "feelin' good."

As the drinking and dancing progressed the guys, emboldened by alcoholic courage, became louder, and more familiar with the girls. Anxious to show their boldness, they would gently slap, and touch their daters in forbidden places. Soon, one by one, couples begin disappearing to explore what mysteries the moonlit night held for them.

Phil and Eileen talked for what seemed like hours getting to know each other. Suddenly they looked up, across the smoke-filled room, to discover they were alone; having been deserted by other couples. Phil placed the empty beer bottle he held on the bar, and turned to Eileen. He noticed she held a half-empty bottle of beer she had been holding all evening. Offering his hand, he asked, "Would you like to go see a small lake, on the Fisher property?"

"Oh, yes; that would be wonderful," she answered.

Leaving the building the cool chill of the night air cleared Phil's head, and sent a shiver through his body.

"Are you cold?" he asked Eileen.

"A little," she answered.

Removing his coat, he said, "Here, take my jacket." He placed it over her shoulders. His hands closed the coat around her. He felt the warmth of her body; they stood motionless under the soft glow of moonlight. His face was inches from hers, when their eyes met. Suddenly, his arms were around her; he found her lips, and passionately kissed her. Resisting at first, she tried to pull away. His arms tightened around, and he pressed his body against hers. Yielding, she slipped her arms around his neck, pressing her body against his. For several minutes, seeming only seconds to Phil, they stood embraced, and then separated. He had been hungry for her kisses.

"You shouldn't have done that," she said.

"I know, but I'm not sorry; are you? He questioned.

"No. I wanted you to," she whispered.

"Let's go see the lake," he suggested, with a voice of encouragement.

They strolled hand in hand down the well-worn path, through the woods, to the edge of the lake.

The full silvery moon reflected the mirror like beauty of the lake as they looked out across the water. It had felt cool when they came out of the stuffy party room, but now, the air drifting toward them, from the earlier sun-bathed lake, was warm on their faces.

"Do you swim?" asked.

"Oh yes; I love it," she answered.

"Let's go swimming," he invited.

"I don't have a bathing suit," she replied.

"Oh, yeah; that," he said. Suddenly realizing when he and Dave swam, they were always nude.

Embarrassed, he blurted out, "Just as minute. I'll be right back." He crossed a short stretch of beach to a small cabin he and Dave had built for fishing. He was thinking of the blankets and matches they kept in the cabin. With a blanket and handful of matches he quickly returned.

"If we don't go swimming, we can at least have a fire and a blanket to lie on," he explained. He spread the blanket out on the sand and collected dry roots and bark to kindle a fire. He could see other fires down the short beach and knew others would be swimming, suit or no suit.

The fire quickly burst into flame. He and Eileen lay side by side. Their bodies touched and his pulse quickened. They lay together enjoying the stillness of the night, and the dancing shadows cast by the fire. Impulsively, he reached out touching Eileen's head. Her breathing quickened when he ran his fingers through her hair, and down her back. He drew her to him, bringing his lips gently down on hers, hoping she would not resist. He held her closer; she placed both arms around his neck.

Cuddling and kissing, they clung together in a warm embrace. Then nervously broke apart, exhausted from controlling their emotions, before surrendering to their passion.

"Let's go swimming and cool off," he suggested.

"But we can't go in naked," she argued softly.

"Why not," he urged. No one will see us and we won't see each other. The fire has burned down to a bed of embers and we won't build it back up," he continued.

"I just can't. What if Pat found out and told my parents?" she questioned.

"Pat will never find out," Phil promised.

"I will, on one condition," Eileen negotiated.

"Name it", Phil said.

"We both go away from the fire, undress, then enter the water at different places. We can come together out in the water at different points and we won't be able to see each other," she explained.

"Ok, agreed," he answered.

They left the fire to undress. Phil stepped out of his shorts and sat down on a log to have a cigarette before the swim. Waiting until he heard Eileen enter the water, he dived in and swam to where he thought she would be. He took a deep breath and dove beneath her and grabbed her legs. They surfaced together laughing. Their lips met as they faced each other.

"There's a little point across the lake about five hundred feet away. Can you see it?" he asked, pointing.

"Yes," she replied

"Let's race out to it and then back to the beach," he suggested.

"Yes. Say when you are ready," she answered.

"Now," he said and they started together. Phil let her get a slight lead and then realized she was an excellent swimmer. She streaked through the water quickly reaching the point. Pausing only to catch her breath she headed back to shore; they passed each other on the way back to the beach. Gaining the lead, he reached shallow water, stood up and offered her his hand to pull her from the lake. They ran to the blanket and lay exhausted from the strenuous exercise. Several minutes passed before she realized she lay naked on the blanket.

Embarrassed she said, "I better get dressed."

"Aw, relax and rest a few minutes," he encouraged and continued, jokingly." Besides, I will close my eyes when I look at you."

"Thanks a bunch," she replied, and with panic in her voice asked, "Oh, what am I going to tell Pat about my wet hair?"

"It will dry before you see her. You worry too much. Here, let me shake the water out and help it to dry." He ran his fingers through her hair; they tingled when he touched her warm body. He raised her chin and again found her lips. Her body trembled as his body pressed against hers.

"We better not," but her words of protest were drowned as his lips again closed over hers. They lay face to face only inches apart. Slowly the distance closed. Phil's hands explored her body; the firmness of her breasts, the smoothness of her thighs. Little sounds of joy escaped her throat. Suddenly, she sprang to her feet.

"What's the matter?" he asked.

"We better get dressed and join the rest of the group," she explained.

"Is your hair dry?" he asked.

"Almost, but I don't have a comb," she said.

"You can use mine," he replied.

Walking back up the trail to the house Phil was ashamed and embarrassed for letting his emotions rule his body. He was thankful to Eileen for not letting them go the "last mile." Looking at his watch he saw that it was almost two in the morning. "What time do you have to be home?" Phil asked.

"No particular time. I'm sleeping over with Pat," she replied.

Entering the party room, they saw others were preparing to leave. Although, some were still in the mood for partying. Dave and Pat came down from upstairs. Dave announced, "Well gals and guys, I guess that just about winds up another one of good ol' Dave's Famous Parties. Sure hope everyone had fun and we can have another blast real soon. So long everybody. Drive safe on the way home." With this announcement couples headed for cars and home.

As the last car pulled from the driveway Dave turned to Phil and Eileen and asked, "Are you folks ready?"

"Yeah we are", said Phil.

Little was said on the way into town and Pat's home. It appeared a mutual understanding existed between the foursome. They drove past Pat's house and parked several houses down the street. Dave and Pat went into a goodnight embrace. Phil turned to Eileen and asked, "When will I see you again?"

"Do you want to?" she surprisingly asked.

"Yes. Of course," he replied, taking her in his arms and kissing her goodnight.

"I was hoping so," she whispered into his ear. "Call me."

"What's your number?" he whispered back. She took a small notepad from her purse and scribbled her number on it.

Dave and Phil patiently waited until their dates silently let themselves into Pat's house, before driving away.

CHAPTER 3

Mischief Makers

At the next meeting of the "Dare Devil Club", plans were completed for Halloween. A list of pranks to avenge the admonitions administered against the pranksters. These young people were not abnormally deviant of character; neither would their acts of mischief fall under the category of juvenile delinquency. Lacking sufficient parental guidance, compassion, and love they sought to express their nervous energy to find amusement. Their environment of a so-called "lower class," forced maturity much too soon. Eager to participate in activities considered normal for adolescents they felt compelled to defend their activities by any possible means.

In acts of ambivalence, the guys and gals had formed a habit of going to an abandoned airstrip to participate in "joy-riding, dragging, and "hot-rodding" as they called it. On a Friday after school several of the guys planned to go to the strip and drag race. Skip Lonigan had bet Keith Duncan a case of beer his "mill" could out-drag Keith's. Each were excited and anxious to win.

Arriving at the location the cars lined up on the far end of the mile-long strip. Each driver settled in the seat of their "mill" and gunned the engine, eager to get underway. Volunteer flagmen took their place, one to signal the start, another to dip the winning flag at the end of a quarter-mile.

All eyes were on the cars; the flag was in the air and fell at the sound of a whistle. Engines roared to life at full throttle tires squealed and each car raced down the strip. Skip shifted, using a daring speed-shift and missed second. Gears clashed before meshing and the Ford Thunderbird jumped forward with blazing speed. Keith made a smooth start with a perfect speed-shift, gears meshing noiselessly. Skip tried to close the gap. A half-car length separated them when the flag at the finish line dropped. Keith won!

The race had taken only minutes to run, but seemed like an eternity to Keith. Breathing a sigh of relief, he slowed, turned, and drove back to pick up his passengers before heading to town and the classmate's favorite drive-in restaurant. He was pleased his "souped-up" Mercury had not let him down. Pulling into the drive-in he noted Skip had followed, and pulled alongside him.

"Nice try, Skip," Keith chided him.

"Aw hell! I'd have won if I hadn't missed second" (gear), he grumbled.

"Well, that's the breaks," Keith replied, "I'll see you for that case of beer Saturday night."

"Don't worry. You'll get it!" he shouted over the squeal of rubber and clash of gears as the Thunderbird disappeared in a cloud of gray smoke.

Dave Fisher and Phil Kingsley pulled in alongside Keith's Merc'. "Nice race, man," Dave said.

"Thanks Dave," Keith said. "I was lucky, I guess."

"Luck, or no luck, I was glad to see you wax him. He's such a blowhard. I can't think of a more smart-aliky guy to see ya' beat. Well, gotta go; see ya' Keith," Dave said.

"Yeah. See you guys. So long," Keith replied.

The week quickly passed. Soon it was Halloween. The club members agreed to meet at the clubhouse around seven o'clock, just when it was getting dark. At ten minutes past seven Phil and Dave arrived. Dave had volunteered to be a driver with his dad's pickup truck for their list of pranks.

Some members had already arrived. Walking into the clubhouse, Phil noted with satisfaction the sky was clouded over; there would be no moon tonight. "Well guys, all plans are in place, so we won't waste time. Let's hop into Dave's pick-up and get on the way," he announced to the eager and ready group.

Their first stop was at Mrs. Moore's place where their plan was to move the outhouse behind the hole. Three of the guys went to the door yelling, "Trick or Treat" while the rest soaped the windows and then quickly ran down a short path leading to where the small outhouse building sat. With several standing on either side it was an easy task to move the outhouse behind the hole so that the front edge, which held the door, was even with the back edge of the hole.

Not knowing how long it would be before someone came from the house to use the "privy" the guys settled themselves behind the barn to wait. In about twenty minutes the door to the house opened; a man carrying a lantern stepped into the blackness of the night. He walked toward the outhouse pausing momentarily to light his pipe. The pranksters watched as he approached the outhouse. From the light of the lantern they could see him reach out to open the door; suddenly he and the lantern disappeared, falling into the hole. A stream of curse words broke the stillness of the night and a loud, bellowing voice screamed "Martha! Martha! Martha!"

The door of the house opened and a worried voice loudly called out, "What's the matter John?"

The guys watched the Moore's predicament a few more minutes and then finally, covering their mouths to keep from laughing out loud, moved on to another prank.

"Come on, you guys, let's get out of here."

The next prank was when they had filled paper bags with human waste, and would go from place to place getting even with the residents who had offended them. They would approach a house, place a bag of waste on the doorstep, knock on the door or ring the doorbell, yell

"Trick or Treat" and strike a match to light the bag on fire, and run away. The innocent resident would open the door, see the fire blazing in their doorway and impulsively stomp on the bag in an attempt to put out the fire. In doing so the waste material would spurt up the victim's leg, and into their shoe or slipper. The guys enjoyed this prank and laughed hilariously.

Pranks such as letting air out of tires, tying knots in sleeves of clothes that had been hung out to dry, soaping windows, putting bags of human waste in mail boxes, and turning over garbage cans kept them busy until the wee hours of the morning. Phil finally decided it was time for the prank on Old Mr. Thompson. He knew there would be a lot of activity involved so it had been best to wait until it had gotten very late.

Parking a short distance from the Thompson farm, they continued on foot. Entering the barn, they begin to pass bales of hay to one another, in brigade fashion, and to stack them against the wall of the barn. Lifting the last bale to the top level, even with the flat roof of the tool shed attached to the barn that had been built to park a tractor and farm equipment.

The plan was to stair-step the bales so they could walk the cow up the steps to get it on top of the flat roof. With the make-shift stairs finished, Phil, sweating heavily from the exertion, led the cow out of the barn and coaxed her up the steps formed by the bales of hay. Because the barn roof was so sharply slanted, they had been forced to put the cow on top of the flat roofed tool shed. Phil led the confused animal onto the roof hoping and praying it would not step through a knot-hole and break a leg.

Having placed the cow on the roof, they then begin to pass the bales of hay back into the barn. Cleaning up the loose strands of hay that had fallen from the bales there was no visible signs as to how the cow got on the roof. They held back laughter as they imagined the expression on old Mr. Thompson's face when he came out to milk and saw his cow standing on top of the barn. They consoled themselves by knowing that in their small community they would hear from neighborhood gossip about how he got the cow down.

It was now near dawn, so with pranks completed, they decided it was time to go home. Luckily for them, it was Saturday with no school.

Phil quietly crept into his room, undressed and climbed into bed beside his brother. He knew he would have to get up early to milk the cow and do the many other chores his father would have set aside for him. Though his body ached with fatigue his mind raced with the thought of getting his driver's license next week, of meeting Eileen again, of getting a job so he could buy a car, and of his father's ailing health. Although his father claimed there was nothing wrong with him, he had lately complained of severe headaches, chills, and discomfort. What if he had to be admitted to the hospital and had to quit work. How we would pay the bills? Even though he had admitted to those ailments to the family he refused to go to a doctor, and neither would he stop drinking.

His mind raced with thoughts of "what ifs." His two older brothers were now married; the family could no longer count on their income. Phil, his two sisters, and one younger brother were the only ones remaining at home. But what about the brother or sister that was on the way? His mother was pregnant again. He pondered these thoughts as he tossed and turned. Finally, he closed his eyes and slept.

The soft voice and gentle hands of his mother awakened him, after what seemed only a few minutes. "Time to get up Phil and milk the cow," she said. He raised his head, and opened his eyes. He slowly raised himself from bed, shaking his head to clear away the fogginess. For a few minutes he sat on the edge of the bed while life raced back into his body. His mother smiled and asked a question to which she already knew the answer, "You were out rather late last night; weren't you?"

Phil returned his mother's smile and nodded his head to her question. He noticed the lines of worry had deepened in her gentle face, since he had last taken a closer look. His thoughts were racing again. He hated his father with a passion but he dearly loved his mother.

"Breakfast will be ready by the time you are," she said leaving the room and quietly closing the door.

Phil finished eating breakfast and went out to milk. Entering the house, he was surprised to see the kitchen was empty. Usually by this time everyone was at the breakfast table even on Saturday and Sunday because of his father's demands. Like Napoleon he believed only a fool needed more than four hours sleep. It was very unusual to not see activity in the house. Phil strained the milk and placed it in the cooler. His mother came back into the kitchen.

"Where's Dad this morning, Mom? Is he not feeling well?" he asked.

"No, Son. Your dad ran a high fever all night. I thought it best not to wake him up. Get your brother and sister up; but tell them to be quiet so as not to awaken him," she requested.

Following his mother's request, he woke up his siblings, cautioning them to be quiet and to not disturb their father. Little activity was present in the Kingsley home that Saturday. Each time Phil looked at his mother she appeared more tired. For the first time he noticed gray sprinkled in her heavy black hair.

Phil's father stayed in bed all day. At six o'clock that evening Phil's mother come to him in the living room as he sat reading and announced, "Your father would like to see you Phil."

Phil wondered what his dad wanted as he arose and walked toward the parent's bedroom. The unmistakable odor of alcohol seemed to literally reek from the walls of the dimly lit room. Although his dad had been in the room less than twenty-four hours, he had not been able to stop drinking the raw 100 proof "white lightnin'".

As Phil stood in the room waiting for his dad to speak, the strong smell of alcohol nearly overwhelmed him. If there had ever been any doubt his suspicions were now confirmed; his father was a full-blown alcoholic.

Moving to the foot of the bed Phil greeted his father. "Hello Dad. How are you feeling?" Without waiting for an answer, he asked, "You wanted to see me?"

"Yes, Son. I'll be ready to go to work Monday. I just got a touch of the flu," he explained. "What I wanted to talk to you about is this. I don't think I will be able to take your mother and the family to church tomorrow. So, I want you to take them in the car," he said.

"But I …" Phil started to interrupt but his father raised his hand to silence him.

"I know you don't have your license yet, but there will be very little traffic and I know you can make it alright. Besides, you are a good driver; I taught you myself, didn't I?" his father joked.

"Ok Dad. I'll do it, if you say so, and they are not afraid to ride with me," Phil said.

"Don't worry, they'll go with you." "Another thing" he continued, "I want you to know that whatever happens to me, I have always tried to be a good father, a good husband and provider to your mother and the family. "Oh sure, I've done a lot of things which I probably shouldn't have, but I've always believed in God and have always tried to see to it that your mother and you kids got to church."

"Sure, you have, Dad, and don't you worry, nothing is going to happen to you. I do think you should go down and see Dr. Anderson just for a checkup," Phil suggested.

"Naw, I'll be all right in a day or so. I don't want to pay no doctor to do what I already know to do; 'kill the germ' that doctor would say. I've already drowned it," he said grinning and motioning to the half-empty jug of clear liquid sitting on a bedside table. "Do that little thing for me and I'll 'preciate it," he said in a tone indicating Phil was dismissed.

"Yes, I will, Dad," Phil replied and quietly left the room.

Phil could not understand his father's sudden interest in church. They family had attended from time to time ever since he could remember but had not been what you would call a religious family. He recalled that many Sundays after church they would have "roast Preacher" at the dinner table. That is, criticizing the preacher for preaching too long, or for something he had said or done.

He didn't particularly have a very fond memory of Sunday School. The teachers had always been inclined to have a pious "better than you" attitude. Or at least he thought so. They never allowed the student an opportunity to voice their opinion or views. They seemed to just teach their own interpretation of the Bible, leaving no room for discussion.

Phil figured this was the reason he had assumed a "take it; or leave it" attitude toward church and had adopted the Epicurean attitude of 'Eat, drink, and be merry, for tomorrow you may die.'" He had promised his father he would drive the family to church, so regardless of his own feelings he would keep the promise.

By Sunday afternoon, Verle Kingsley was feeling better. He drank some beef broth and ate chicken soup. As predicted, he returned to work on Monday. While still pale and weak, his determination was greater than his common sense.

Phil's memory was stirred from the church visit. He began to recall one thing he did remember. About how to become a Christian. His teacher taught the class how to repent of their sin, and invite Christ into their heart as personal savior. Which, according to the Bible, assured one of a life beyond physical life; Eternal life.

Phil remembered at an early age he had believed that, had made that commitment, and was baptized. He also remembered how the teacher taught "when a Christian believer dies a physical death, the spirit goes home to be with the Lord." She had pointed to a Scripture confirming her teaching. He had never forgotten that Scripture, and let it refresh his memory: "to be absent from the body, is to be present with the Lord." II Corinthians 5:8." Phil still believed this and planned to share it with his best friend Dave who was Catholic. So that, if he had never done so he too, could make that commitment.

CHAPTER 4

Teenage Tragedy

The week before Phil was to take the driver's examination, while filled with activities, seemed to drag by. He went to a couple of schoolmate drag races but was unable to show the enthusiasm and interest he usually enjoyed. He couldn't concentrate on studies and caught himself looking out the window at school daydreaming. Friday, the seemingly longest day of all, finally came. Anxiously waiting for the school dismissal bell to ring his eyes were glued to the hands of the big clock on the wall wishing the hours away. The bell finally rang. He sprinted from the classroom and headed toward Dave's car in the parking lot.

Lost in thought, he suddenly remembered some of the classmates had a wiener roast planned for tonight, down at Sage Beach which was about 20 miles from town. With dismay he also remembered he had not invited Eileen to go with him. He frantically looked through his wallet searching for her phone number. As he slid into the passenger seat, Dave asked him, "What ya' looking for, man?".

"Eileen's phone number," Phil replied.

"Ya' plan on takin' her to the roast?" he asked.

"Yes. If I'm not too late in askin'", Phil answered.

"She's been out of town to some relative's funeral. A least that's what Pat told me," he explained. "Let's roll out to Pat's and see if she knows if Eileen is back home."

Pulling up in front of Pat's home they saw Pat going up the walk. Dave blasted the horn. Pat turned, waved, and came running to the car.

"Hi guys. What's happening?" she greeted them.

"Hi Baby," Dave said.

"Hello Pat," Phil also greeted her.

Dave continued, "Hey Sweets, Phil wants to ask you a question."

Looking at Phil she replied, "Ask away."

"I was wondering if Eileen has come home yet. I'm going to invite her to the wiener roast," Phil said.

"I don't know. She was not in school today. But let's go in and call her." Pat suggested.

They waited while Pat rummaged through her bag for the key. Phil wondered why the door would be locked if the parents were inside. He later learned both of her parents worked.

Entering the living room Phil was impressed by the beautiful furnishings. A secret desire jumped into his mind and he told himself that he would one day own a home like this.

Pat went to the phone and dialed Eileen's number. Her mother answered the phone. "Hello Mrs. Marshall. Is Eileen there? If so, may I speak to her, please?" She asked. After a brief pause Pat said, "Hi Eileen. Someone here would like to talk to you. Guess. No. No, here, I'll let you talk to him," she said, handing the phone to Phil.

Dave and Eileen walked into the kitchen while Phil spoke with Eileen. "Hi Eileen", Phil greeted her.

"Hi yourself", she said, "Who is this?"

"It's Phil. I'm sorry to learn about your family member loss. My condolences. It's good that you're back home."

"I just got home a little while before Pat called," she replied.

"How's that for timing?" Phil joked.

"Yeah, it seems like you do have a way of being in the right place at the right time," she joked back, her mind racing to their first date. "What's on your mind?" she asked.

"How about going to a wiener roast with me tonight out at Sage Beach?" he invited.

"Well, I don't know. I'm awfully tired," she teased.

"Aw, come on. You're not that tired. Besides you can rest up at the roast," he persisted.

"Well… alright. Actually, I wouldn't miss it for the world," she said, accepting the invitation.

"Thanks. Wear something casual, and bring a jacket," he suggested.

"Are we going swimming?" she laughingly asked.

His face turned red with embarrassment. "Probably not. The tide will be going out by the time we get there. We'll be picking you up around seven, if that's ok with you," he said more seriously.

"That's good with me," she replied. See ya' then. Bye Phil," she said and hung up the phone.

A little past seven Dave, Pat, and Phil pulled up in front of Eileen's home. It had already been a long day for Phil. After school he had milked the cow, chopped wood, and finished a couple of other chores before taking a bath and eating.

With three short blasts of the horn Dave, Pat, and Phil pulled into Eileen's driveway. Eileen came to the door and called out to "Come on in, folks. Mother and Daddy want to meet Phil."

Phil felt self-conscious as he entered the Marshall home. Making a quick mental assessment of his appearance and reassured himself he was properly dressed. He decided her parents couldn't be too critical. After all, they were going on a beach party wiener roast. Eileen was wearing very tight black slacks, and a white turtleneck sweater. Phil noticed the slacks revealed her shapely figure. From the waist up, he imagined she looked like a contestant from a "Miss Sweater Girl" Contest.

"Mother, Daddy, this is Phil Kingsley, and of course you know Pat and Dave," she said introducing Phil.

Phil could see Eileen was almost like a clone of her mother. Mrs. Marshall was just as shapely as her daughter. Maturity added to her attractiveness.

"Hello Phil, Eileen has said so much about you. I feel like I already know you," she greeted him.

Phil flashed an easy smile saying, 'I'll try to live it down,' and acknowledged her friendly handshake.

"Oh, it really wasn't bad," Eileen said, blushing with laughter.

"I was just kidding," Phil replied smiling again.

"Daddy, meet Phil Kingsley,

"How do you do Sir," Phil asked, accepting the extended hand of Eileen's father.

"I'm good, real good," he answered, and continued, "Let's not keep the kids from their beach party."

"Yes. We gotta' be going," Pat said, breaking her silence.

"Nice meeting you, Phil," Mrs. Marshall said. "And you kids have fun, but be careful, and safe out there", as the couples returned to the car.

They passed several other carloads of couples on the road leading to Sage Beach.

Dave, always in a hurry, was in even bigger hurry tonight. He knew that there were only few good spots with fire pits on the beach and he was anxious to be one of the first to arrive so they could have their choice and claim one of the best spots.

One of the couples they passed was Skip Lonigan and his girlfriend, Doris. Skip recognizing Dave's car, put the throttle to the metal shifting into second gear. As jets of fuel fed into the twin carburetors, the Thunderbird responded and took off like a shot. Dave, realizing what was happening, shifted his fairly new Oldsmobile, into second gear and jammed down his foot on the gas pedal. They hung neck and neck. The Old's begin to take the lead.

Dave knew the Thunderbird with only twin carbs and milled heads would be no match for the Old's. With a ¾ Camshaft, twin Carbs, and racing heads, the Old's was well in the lead when he shifted from second at seventy miles per hour. The road, while secondary, was fairly straight and in good repair. Dave let up on the accelerator at ninety miles per hour and settled back to a good, smooth eighty-five. He glanced in the rearview mirror and was pleased to see Skip's headlights far in the rear.

Arriving at the beach they could already see bonfires burning. Showers of sparks and ashes sailed skyward as more fuel was added to fires. The sparks and ash seemed to mingle with the sun's rays as it slowly sank in the ocean. They rolled onto the hard-packed sand and drove to a stretch of smooth, white sand sheltered by a little cove. It was a perfect spot.

The shelter of the cove provided plenty of protection against the smoke from bonfires. A fire pit sat in the middle of the sheltered spot. The white sand offered illumination on this night; a night that promised a very dim moon.

Dave and Phil unloaded Presto Logs, wieners, buns, condiments, and beer from the car, while Pat and Eileen spread blankets over the hard- packed sand, around an area surrounded by stones.

Phil brought logs to the fire pit, spread newspapers and shavings in the bottom of the pit, placing logs on top, sprayed lighter fluid over the logs, and set it on fire. The logs quickly caught fire and begin to burn brightly.

Dave opened a round of beers. Phil joined them where they lay sprawled on blankets waiting for the fire to burn down to a bed of coals, before roasting wieners. Phil lay beside Eileen facing the sea, listening to the sound of waves crashing on the shore. She reached for his hand, "Isn't it lovely?" she whispered, referring to the moon beginning its slow ascent. The moon's normal brightness was dimmed by a misty halo, while it nudged its way skyward.

"It sure is. Makes you want to forget who you are, and where you are, and just be thankful you are alive," he replied.

Lying serene on the beach they felt at peace with the world. The sound of waves filled the night, majestically rolling beach ward and crashing on the shore. A fine mist of salt spray moistened their cheeks when the waves ended, and rolled back into the sea.

Dave and Pat were holding roasting forks. Kneeling by the fire, they began to roast wieners. Phil and Eileen joined them, also roasting wieners. They watched them sizzle, sputter, and start to curl from the heat. A tangy, delicious aroma filled the air when the wieners turned a crispy brown. Phil and Eileen momentarily turned their attention from each other to enjoy the tantalizing taste of hot dogs smothered with onions, covered with mustard, making them tastier by munching on dill pickles. Their thoughts imagined the simple food, seemingly improved by the fresh salt air, was fit for a king!

The couples munched on hot dogs and, between bites washed them down with cold beer. Having eaten their fill of hot dogs they returned to lay on the blankets smoking cigarettes, joking, laughing, drinking beer and having a fun time.

Tiring of banter, conversation soon turned to a more serious subject. "Phil, what are you going to do after high school?" Eileen asked.

"I don't know. I haven't really given it too much thought," he replied. "What about you?"

"I've always wanted to be a nurse. Mother wants me to go to acting school and become an actress. She gave up an acting career when she married Daddy and has been a little resentful of it and wants to try and live her life through me, I think. She and Daddy are not very happy together," she related.

"That's too bad," Phil empathized.

"Not really. It's just that Mother wants her way all of the time and Daddy is becoming henpecked. This bothers me because I hate to see a henpecked husband. I want to see one who knows what he wants, and knows how to obtain it," she said pressing Phil's hand.

He knew what she meant. "I don't know which is worse; a henpecked husband or a henpecked wife," he said remembering his own mother and father's unhappy family situation.

While they talked, loud voices and the sound of breaking glass drifted down the beach toward them.

"They must be having a ball down there," Phil said, starting to get up. Eileen pulled him back down on the blanket. "That's their business, let's keep our fun down here," she said leaning toward him. It was getting cooler and darker. The moon slid behind the clouds. He sought and found her lips in the darkness and felt the gentleness of her hands as they cradled his cheeks. The warmth of her body stirred his passion when she snuggled to him and tightly held him.

Abruptly, loud sounds of car doors slamming and hysterical female screams shattered the night. Phil and Eileen jumped to their feet. They knew from the all too familiar sounds; a fight was in progress further down the beach.

"Dave! Dave!", Phil called out."

"Yeah?" a muffled voice replied.

"Let's go down and stop the fight," Phil suggested.

"Aw, hell, let 'em fight it out," Dave replied.

Phil was disappointed in Dave's response. He knew Dave was very influential and could have stopped the fight. Phil had heard of these beach fights and knew they could be dangerous especially if weapons were involved.

Phil was pleased when the noise died down leaving only the sound of waves thundering against the shore. Phil and Eileen tried to recapture the fervor of their passion but discovered it had melted away with the hysterical screams in the night. They lay in each other's arms and finally dozed.

Pat's voice saying, "Time to go," awoke them in the early morning hours.

"Gosh, we must have dozed off, what time is it?" he asked, getting up.

"Past 2 AM," she answered.

Phil helped Dave and Pat load up the car with the leftover food items. While they worked, they could hear other partygoers preparing to leave. Horns honked, doors slammed, and cold engines roared to life, dual exhausts muffled by the sand. After necessary preparation they climbed into the car. The chilly hours caused them to huddle close to their companion, trying to stay warm, until the heater kicked in rushing warmth into the interior of the car.

Driving to the highway entrance, they saw several cars sitting idling while drivers talked. Dave recognized Skip Longing, who in turn, recognized Dave. And he called out. "Hey, man, that was pretty cool the way you waxed me. You wouldn't have done it if my twin pots hadn't a been messin' up."

"Well, I'll try you another time and see if ya make out," Dave taunted him.

"Yeah. Ok, but in the meantime, how about playin' a game on the way home?"

"What kinda' game?" Dave asked.

"The game of chicken," Skip said.

"I've heard of it. How do you play it?" Dave questioned.

"Here's the way we're gonna play it," Skip answered. "About five cars are gonna drive down the road about fifteen miles, turn around, kill their headlights, and drive down the center strip at seventy miles per hour. After seeing another car coming at ya', the first one to pull out of the way is "chicken", Skip explained.

"Sounds pretty silly; a dangerous game, if you ask me. It's like committing suicide," Phil responded in a disgusted voice.

"Aw, hell. You're just chicken already!" Skip retorted.

Pulling back on to the road they could hear Skip yelling instructions to those who planned to play the "game."

Before driving back to town, Dave was pondering whether to drive fast to avoid the game-players, or drive slow to let the players, who in his mind were deciding on a pathway to suicide, know he was not a participant. He decided on the latter.

Driving the thirty-five miles per hour speed limit, cars zoomed around him, speeding on down the highway, taillights fading in the distance.

"Those must be the ones who will turn around, and come back down the center line without lights," Dave said to the others.

"Yeah, that's the craziest thing I ever heard of. They are really anxious to die young," Phil replied, remembering the long "S" curve closer to town, commonly called "dead man's corner". He shivered at the thought.

They had driven about fifteen miles when cars without lights, and with drivers straining forward to see the darkened highway, sped toward them. The cars without lights swung out of the center of the highway when they passed, and moved back onto the center white line to guide them.

Suddenly out of nowhere a pair of bright lights flashed on behind them. Dave's hand moved to cover the rearview mirror, shielding his eyes from the blinding reflection. The car behind closed in on their bumper and stayed there. The driver becoming impatient swung around them and pulled alongside Dave's car. Skip's face leering at them laughed loudly and yelled "Chicken! Chicken! Chicken!" Punching the accelerator, he sped on by them moving back into the center of the road, with headlights going black when Skip turned off the lights.

"Doris looked scared," Pat said.

"Can you blame her? If her parents knew they would never let her go out with Skip again," he said.

"He'll never learn," Phil said. "He may get older but never smarter. There's no fix for stupid. It must have been people like him the old German philosopher was lookin' at when he said 'Ve get old so soon; and schmart so late.'"

"He probably won't even remember it tomorrow. He looked pretty drunk to me," Eileen said.

"Oh, he'll remember alright. He'll be bragging to everybody about he was the only one who didn't chicken out," Phil said.

Approaching town, they could see lights in the distance. Dave knew they were not far away. He breathed a sigh of relief, recognizing car after car passing them going in the opposite direction, with lights turned on. They must have been the ones who "chickened out."

The cool of the early morning hour became colder as they picked up speed thinking the game of "chicken" was over. Dave leaned forward to close the vents and roll up his window when the thunderous crash of metal against metal shattered the stillness.

"Sounds like someone didn't make it," Phil said as they approached Dead Man's Corner.

Reaching the sharpest part of the curve, they could see Skip's Thunderbird laying upside down with wheels still spinning. Their headlights picked up the outline of a large vehicle with a crushed front-end laying on its side next to the Thunderbird. Stopping the car, they quickly got out to see if they could help the occupants. Other cars, the more fortunate game players, were also stopping as "looky-loos" to see the tangled, and twisted mass of the two wrecked cars.

Doris's body had been thrown clear, at the point of impact. Skip was pinned in the vehicle by the steering wheel, which appeared to have caved in his chest. Lying on his back in an upside down position as blood ran from his nose and mouth, matting his hair to his head. From where she lay, Doris groaned with pain.

The lone occupant of the other car involved was walking around as if in a dazed stupor saying over and over, "Oh, my God! What have I done? What have I done?"

Observing the situation, Dave said, "We better call the police and an ambulance."

"Yeah. Not much we can do here," Phil agreed.

"We'll stop at the first phone booth to call," Dave said. He helped Pat and Eileen, both who were nauseated, back into the car. Within half a mile they found a service station with a public phone booth. Jumping from the car Dave first called an ambulance, and then the police to report the accident. Getting back in the car he felt sick to his stomach having had to relate details of the accident to the operator.

"Do you think we should go back?" Phil asked.

Dave said, "No, Phil. We better get you home. If your dad ever finds out you were anywhere near this accident, he would never let you get your license, or trust you out with the car."

In less than ten minutes, they saw a police car followed by an ambulance, with Sirens screaming, race by on way to the accident.

"Don't anyone breathe a word of this that we were near this accident, or we'll never be able to stay out past midnight," Dave cautioned. "If anyone asks you about it, tell them all you know is what you read in the newspaper."

Dropping off Pat and Eileen, Dave drove to Phil's home.

Dawn was breaking when Phil got out of the car, and said good night to Dave.

CHAPTER 5

An Exciting Venture

It seemed to Phil, no sooner had his head hit the pillow than he was awakened by his mother. "Time to get up, Son. You brother is even milking the cow for you, so you and Dad can get an early start into town," she said.

Phil shook his head to clear away the cobwebs and rubbed sleep from his eyes. "Ok. Thanks Mom, I'll be right out," he answered.

He noticed his mother was getting heavier with pregnancy. That aside he suddenly remembered today was the day he was going to get his driver's license. He had just finished breakfast when his father came into the kitchen. "About ready, Phil?"

"I sure am, Dad," he replied.

"Let's get going then," his dad said.

Phil was nervous, and uneasy, but excited, as they drove to the state police station office. He was not unsure of his ability to pass the driving exam but nervous about the fact his father had recently installed a new clutch in the car and he had not driven the car enough to become familiar with it. This coupled with his nervousness, might lessen his chance for a good showing. Reaching the station, they went inside to be waited on by a sergeant behind the desk. Explaining the reason for the visit, the sergeant handed Phil a written exam to complete before the driving test.

Having finished the written exam, he handed it to the sergeant, who graded the exam. Phil was pleased to note, he had missed the correct answer to only one question. The burley sergeant came out from behind the desk, and made a big show of pulling up his trousers, and tucking in his shirt. "Come on. Son. Let's go for the driving test," he said.

Leaving the office, they walked to the parking lot. "Which car?" the sergeant asked.

"Over here," Phil motioned.

Climbing into the car Phil was about to start the engine. "Just a minute," the Sergeant said. "We are going to pull out, go down Main Street, make a few turn, park the car, and then return to the station. Are you all set?" he asked.

"Yes," Phil replied.

Starting the engine, he let the clutch out slowly, but the car jerked going backwards and bumped into a steel flagpole, before Phil got it under control. He straightened the wheels and prepared to exit the parking lot into Main Street.

"Be careful going out of here, there's a drop off," the sergeant cautioned.

"Ok," Phil replied. Still unfamiliar with the new clutch adjustment, the car was in motion before Phil was ready. Instead of "taking it easy" the car bounced heavily over the drop off onto the street.

Phil noticed the officer writing on the pad he held in his lap and was embarrassed by his obvious blunder, especially after the officer's warning. The sergeant seemed unmoved by the incident and continued to make notations on the pad. Finally, after a series of turns, lane changes and a painful experience of parking, the sergeant told Phil to return to the station. After a proper signal he turned into the parking lot, remembering to be careful over the uneven pavement, and parked the car.

Climbing out of the car the sergeant said to Phil, "Let's go inside." Phil followed not knowing whether he had passed the driving test. The sergeant handed the written report to the duty officer and ordered him to "process it," and disappeared into an office marked "Private, Sgt. Shane."

The duty officer hastily scrutinized the written notations on the report, added a few of his own, and announced, "That'll be twenty dollars."

Phil could not restrain a sigh of relief and quickly handed the officer the money.

"Here is your temporary license. The permanent one will be mailed to you in a week to ten days," the officer explained.

"Thank you," Phil said accepting the license handed to him across the desk.

He could not believe it. At last he held the coveted piece of paper in his hands. Enjoying a feeling of elation, he joined his father in the waiting room and exclaimed, "I made it, Dad!"

"Congratulations Son. I knew you would. You had a good teacher," he jokingly said.

Little was said on the way home, each engrossed in their own thoughts. Phil wondered what the extent of damage was, as a result of last night's accident. Was Skip dead? And what about Doris? He was anxious to see the newspaper account to find out what had really happened.

Driving into the yard he saw Dave's car parked in the driveway. When the car stopped Dave came out to meet them.

"Hi Mr. Kingsley, how are ya'?" Dave asked.

"Fine. Just fine; and yourself", he asked.

"I'm great, thanks," he said and turned to Phil. "How'd you make out, man?"

"I made it, Dave. I am now a fully qualified driver, and have a license to prove it," he replied waving the license for Dave to see.

"Congratulations, man. Congratulations!" Dave said, shaking Phil's hand and slapping him on the back.

Turning to Mr. Kingsley he asked, "Say, have you seen the paper Mr. Kingsley?"

"No. No I haven't. Why do you ask?"

"There was a big wreck on Sage Beach Road last night. Some of the kids Phil and I go to school with were involved," he explained.

"Is that right? Who? "Phil innocently asked.

"Ya' remember Skip Lonigan and his girlfriend Doris? Well, Skip is dead. Doris is in the hospital in serious condition," Dave informed them.

"The young devils were probably doped up with drugs", Verle speculated.

"The paper didn't say," Dave replied. Turning to Phil he said," By the way, Phil, Pat and I are going to the hospital to see Doris. Wanna come along?"

"Can I go Dad?" Phil asked.

"Well, alright. Just be back in time for milking," he answered.

"Thanks, Dad," Phil said. To Dave he said, "Just a minute. I wanna tell Mom about my passing the driver's test and getting my license."

As Phil started toward the house Dave called out, "Ok, but step on it, will ya? I don't want to keep Pat waiting."

Phil noticed Dave and his dad were still talking. He marveled at Dave's ability to carry on a meaningful conversation with older adults. Phil's mother was in the kitchen when Phil ran into the house and announced his success in passing the driving rest and getting his license.

"Wonderful, Son. Congratulations! I had every confidence you would pass," she said.

"Thanks, Mom. I gotta go now. Dave, Pat, and I are going to see one of Pat's friend in the hospital," he explained.

"All right, Son. Be careful and stay safe," she encouraged him.

"I will Mom", he said as he bolted from the kitchen.

"Well, take care of yourself, Mr. Kingsley," Dave said to Phil's father, and climbed into the car with Phil. Backing out of the drive they headed to Pat's place.

"What's the matter with your dad, Phil?' he asked.

"I don't know. Why do you ask?" Phil questioned.

"He doesn't look the same. He looks like he has lost a lot of weight, his eyes look sunken, and he doesn't act like he feels good," Dave replied.

"He has something wrong with him. He claims its rheumatism. Try as we might we can't get him to go the doctor for a checkup," Phil explained.

"He sure oughta' go," Dave emphasized, "Might be something serious."

"I know. We can't get him to listen to reason," Phil replied.

Arriving at Pat's home, and pulling in the driveway, they watched as Pat ran out to meet them.

"Are you ready to go?" Dave asked.

"Yes. Let me lock up the house. I'll be right back."

Little conversation passed between them while driving to the hospital. Each thinking it could have been them or Doris, in Skip's place. They were silently thanking their lucky stars they had not been drunk enough to accept the challenge of the suicidal game of "chicken". Phil wondered was this God trying to get their attention. Was this in some way a providential warning? He also wondered if a police chaplain had been dispatched to the accident. Knowing Skip was a Catholic he would have wanted Last Rites if he thought he was going to die. He dismissed the thoughts from his mind.

Arriving at the hospital they went to the Information Desk to find out the location of Doris. They learned she was in the Intensive Care Unit (ICU). Moving to the ICU they learned visitation was restricted to family only. Finding Doris's family members in the ICU waiting room, taking turns to see her, they identified themselves as Doris' classmates and offered empathy, and prayers for a quick recovery.

Some time passed since Phil received his driver's license. He had become aware it was costing him much more money to live ever since. Not only did he have the cost of entertainment but the added cost of gasoline when he borrowed the family car. He anxiously looked forward to the day he could have his own car, and wondered how he could start earning money to buy it. He realized he would have to get a part-time job. But what? He had no experience in any area of work? He liked cars and decided to look for a job in a service station. He searched the Help Wanted Columns daily but couldn't find a match.

Driving home from school one day he decided to stop by to see a friend he had become acquainted with. The new friend, Clay Roberts, owned a service station and garage. Phil had been using the station to buy gas for the pickup. He pulled into the station. Clay recognized him, waved, and came out to the gas pumps. "Hi Phil. How goes it?" he asked.

"I'm good, Clay. I don't need any gas today. I just wanted to drop by and visit," Phil replied. "How is business?"

"Glad you dropped by. It's been slow on the garage side, but I've been selling a lots gas," he answered.

"You were sayin' the other day you were planning on keeping the station open every night until nine o'clock. Anything new with that?" Phil asked.

"As a matter of fact, yes I am. I plan to start next week. I was getting ready to run an ad tomorrow, now that you ask. Are you lookin' for work?" he asked.

"Yes, I am," Phil replied, getting excited.

"Have you had any service station experience, Phil?" he asked.

"No, I haven't. But I know quite a bit about cars. I'm a quick learner, and I'm willing to learn," Phil said.

"That's a good attitude, Phil," Clay responded. "I'll be able to use you. The pay won't be much to start, but it will increase as you gain experience," Clay informed him.

"Great! I sure appreciate it," Phil replied.

"What time do you get out of school, Phil?" Clay asked.

"I get out of school at 3:30. I could start at four o'clock if that would work," he answered. "That will give me a chance to grab a bite to eat."

"Perfect. I will be expecting you at four then. The first day I'll spend some time with you for orientation."

"Thanks Clay. I'll see ya' then," Phil replied.

Phil was very pleased with himself on the way home. He knew his father would also be pleased now that he had a job and would be able to start paying a little of the household expense. He also knew his younger brother would be unhappy because it would now be his responsibility to do the milking. He smiled in satisfaction as he neared home. It seemed like everything was going his way. He had his driver's license and now a job. He was very pleased and felt good all over.

His mother was preparing dinner when he arrived. His father was sitting in the living room talking to a stranger. He was disappointed he could not talk to his dad because of the stranger's presence. The stranger stood up when Phil entered the room. "All right, Mr. Kingsley, the place will be ready for you in two weeks," the man said.

"Very good, Mr. Moore; we'll be ready for it," his father replied, they shook hands and the stranger left.

"Hi, Dad," Phil said. "I have something important to tell you."

"Ok, you tell me, then I have something to tell you," his father said.

"I have a job, starting Monday," Phil said.

"Doin' what?" his father asked.

"At a service station," Phil replied.

"Good, Son. I'm glad to see you are trying to make something of yourself," his father said. "Now I have something to tell you. We're gonna' move."

"Move! Where?"

"Your mother and I have decided to trade our farm for a little house on the outskirts of town," his father replied. "You'll like it. It's completely modern."

"When do we move?" Phil asked.

"In two weeks. You'll have to start helping your Mother pack all our things," he said.

Phil could hardly believe it. They had lived in this house for twenty years. It didn't seem possible they could be moving. Gradually the shock wore off and he became accepting of the move and even looked forward to it.

The following Monday Phil reported to the new job. His boss spent time with him, teaching him the details of the business and to get him familiar with the steady flow of customers, as well as, to see how he was going to work out. After the first week on the job Phil had adapted well to the customer service of pumping gas, lubricating cars, changing oil and filters, and other duties of a service station attendant. After the second week Clay called him into his office. "Phil, you are doing real well. I'm going to give you keys to the station and let you start closing at night for me."

"Thank you, Clay. I appreciate your confidence in me," Phil replied.

Clay continued with instructions. "One thing I want to caution you about. If anyone tries to rob you, don't resist. We have insurance to cover robberies. Whoever tries to stick you up, give them anything they want," Clay said in a serious voice. On a lighter note he jokingly said, "If they want the gas pumps, get a wrench and help them remove them."

"Ok, Clay, I'll do it if you say so," Phil said in agreement.

The weeks passed in a whirlwind of activity with school, his new job, helping his mother with the packing and multiple other things to do. Before he realized it, they were comfortably settled in the new home. He was pleased with all the conveniences the home offered with the tiled bathroom with shower, and the air conditioning and automatic heat. Phil was amazed at his father's business ability and knowledge which his father called, "'horse tradin'". He wondered if their twenty acre "farm," with ten acres of heavy forest, was worth as much as this fine new home his father had traded for "even up."

Phil's night life had all but disappeared because of his working hours. Being tired after work he had been spending a lot of time at home resting. Saturday evening of the third week working his mother prepared a sandwich and soup for him when he got home.

"Hello, Son, are you tired?" she asked.

"No. Not really, Mom. Why do you ask?"

"Do you have to work tomorrow?" she asked.

"Yes. I guess I'll be working every Sunday. Why, Mom"?

"I haven't said anything to you, Son, but your brother, sisters, and I have joined the local church here in town. We would like to have you come worship with us this Sunday," she explained.

"Naw, I'm afraid I won't have time, Mom. I want to make good on this job and I just don't think the boss will let me off, even to go to church," he protested, not really wanting to go.

"Well, Son, the Bible says, 'To do all thy work in six days; to remember the Sabbath, to keep it holy', she quoted to him.

"I know, Mom. I just don't think I can get off," he replied

"Don't you think your boss would think more of you if you asked him for time off to attend church?" she insisted.

"No. He likes to sleep in on Sunday and I don't think he would appreciate it." he countered.

"Ok, Son. Have it your way," she said in a sad voice, and left the room.

Phil was wondering. What is this? That people seem to think I need religion. I have always tried to do the right thing with others. I have tried to pay my way, share expenses no matter what I and others were doing. Even if we were going on a beer bust or an all-night party. I've always tried to be fair and honest. Maybe I haven't always done the right thing, but I've always paid my way. Phil's thoughts were troubling him. In bed that night he tossed and turned until sleep finally came.

CHAPTER 6

Night of Self Deception

Time marched swiftly by for Phil. Suddenly, school was over. His mind turned to romance. He remembers someone had once said "In Spring, (or was it Summer), a young man's fancy lightly turns to thoughts of love." His thoughts were turning to love as he imagined himself pulling up to Eileen's home in his own car. He was pleased to think about what a wonderful time they would share this summer.

By the time school was let out he had saved quite a bit of money toward the purchase of a car. He was glad his father had consented to co-signing on a loan. He searched the Want Ads in the newspaper for cars for sale. One ad mentioned a used, repossessed Cadillac convertible. His pulse quickened when he read, and re-read, the advertisement description:

> "Need responsible party to take over
> Payments on late model Cadillac
> Convertible. Full power; immaculate
> Condition throughout."

"Why not?" he asked himself. He had always dreamed of owning a big, flashy car and here was his chance, if he could swing it. He went to the phone and called the dealer.

"Good afternoon, Winter Motors. How can I help you?" the operator asked.

"I'm calling about the Cadillac convertible you have advertised. Is it still available?" Phil replied.

"Hold on please, I'll connect you to a sales person", she said.

"This is Jeff speaking. How can I help you?" the sales person's voice enquired.

"I'm calling about the Cadillac convertible you have advertised, "Phil repeated.

"Yes. Thank you for calling. That's really a jewel of a car with low mileage," the sales person answered.

"What's the story on the car?" Phil asked.

"It's a repo, the owner defaulted on the loan and the car came back to Winter Motors," the sales person explained.

"The ad says 'take over payments.' What does that mean?" Phil asked.

"There is such a low balance the dealer made a decision not to refinance the loan. Rather, to let a responsible party assume the loan with a promissory note, and take over the payments."

"How much are the payment, and what is the balance due?" Phil asked, trying to mask the excitement in his voice.

"I really should not be sharing this information by phone, Sir. If you are really interested please come on down to Winter Motors and we can discuss it with you."

"Ok. Thank you for answering my call. I hope to be down tomorrow, Phil replied.

"Good. I'm sure you'll fall in love with this car," the sales person enthusiastically said.

The next day, Saturday, he didn't have to go to work until four o'clock. So, knowing they would have plenty of time to shop, he asked his father if he would go with him to look for a car to buy. His father agreed and they started looking at different makes and models. Secretly

Phil was not interested in any of them. He had his mind set on looking at the Cadillac convertible he had called about. He finally steered his dad to Winter Motors. The salesman was right. He fell in love with the car the moment he set eyes on it. The gleaming chrome was blinding as it caught the noonday sun, reflecting it back into their eyes.

"Let's look at this one, Dad," Phil suggested with excitement.

"Aw, Son, ya' don't want anything this fancy or expensive," his dad discouraged him.

"It doesn't cost anything to look. Let's just look at this one, Dad," Phil pleaded.

"Well, awright' but it's much too rich for your blood," his father explained.

While they talked, a smiling sales person appeared from nowhere and introduced himself. My name is Tony," he said as they walked toward the Cadillac convertible. Noticing the glint in Phil's eye he began to praise the Cadillac, "This is a real beauty."

"How much you askin' for it?" Phil asked.

"This is a repo (repossession) Sir. We are asking for a responsible party to just take over the payments with a Promissory Note," he answered.

"How much are the payments?" Phil asked.

"I have the paperwork in my office, Sir. If you're interested, we can step into the office," he invited.

"Yes. I'm interested. Dad, can we go with Tony to find out the details?" Phil asked his father.

"Sure, Son, if you really are interested", his father replied.

Inside the office, Tony pulled up the paperwork and said, "The payments are $70 per month."

Phil was doing some fast calculating. He earned $40 a week, or $160 a month. His only fixed expense was the payment to his parents of $40 a month for room and board.

Becoming even more excited, he reasoned he could afford to buy the Cadillac. If only his dad didn't object. But why would he? He would be paying for the car himself. His dad wouldn't have to be responsible, even though he would be a co-signer on the promissory note, he would not be having to pay out any money.

"What do you think, Dad?" Phil asked.

His father turned to Tony and asked, "What's the balance?"

"It has a ridiculously low balance of just $2,895," Tony answered. "It's a good buy at twice the price."

Looking at Phil, his father said, "That's an awful lot of money, Son."

"But Sir, this is a lotta' car," Tony interrupted and rebutted the argument with a ready reply.

Phil again turned to his father and asked, "What do you think, Dad?"

"It's your money, Son. If this is what you want. It's your money," he repeated.

"Would you like to drive the car, Sir?" Tony asked Phil.

"Yes. I would," Phil answered.

"The keys are in it. Take it for a spin," Tony invited.

"Let's try it, Dad," Phil urged his father.

The big engine roared as it came to life settling to a smooth purr. Phil could feel a surge of power when he accelerated and exited the sales lot, turning into the main street. It was like nothing he had ever experienced. The way the car handled, the quiet way it ran, and the instant response to the lightest touch of the throttle. The fact that the top was down gave a feeling of freedom. It was exactly what he wanted. He had never wanted anything so much as he wanted this car.

They returned to the dealer and completed the transition. Ready to drive home Phil felt like a king. He thanked his father for coming with him and for co-signing for the car. His chest swelled with pride when he slid behind the steering wheel and headed for work.

If only some of those people, who had told him he would never amount to anything, could only see him now! His thoughts racing, he imagined their eyes would bulge with envy! Here he was, just a kid in high school, working almost full time, driving a Cadillac! In his mind he could hear them saying, "Man, look! There goes that Kingsley kid driving a Cadillac! He really must be loaded with dough!"

Clay was surprised when Phil pulled into the station. "Man, I must be payin' you too much, if you can afford to drive somethin' like his," he said, jokingly.

"What do you think, Clay?' Phil asked.

"It looks great, Phil. Drive it into the garage and we'll run some tests on her," he suggested.

Phil pulled the car into the garage and Clay got busy running routine checks on the engine, front end alignment, transmission, etc. Completing the last test Clay said to Phil, "Looks like you picked a winner. She's in great shape."

"Thanks, Clay. I was pretty sure she was," Phil said.

"You have a real fine buggy here," Clay assured him. "She'll give you a lot of trouble-free service."

True to his expectation, Phil was the most popular, and talked about guys in school for weeks to come. The girl's oooohed and aaahed; some of the guys turned green with envy. Dave Fisher was one of the first to congratulate him. "Boy, this is really some mill' Eileen will flip when she sees this," Dave said admiringly.

"No kidding man! Do you really like it?' Phil asked.

"Do I like it, man? Tell me, do cows give milk," Dave sarcastically retorted. They both laughed at the obvious answer.

Phil truly enjoyed the gasps of his classmates as they stared in awe when he passed them.

The next Saturday after work Phil had a date with Eileen. He hadn't seen her since the night of the party at Sage Beach. He wanted to surprise her with his new car when he went to pick her up for the date. He had spent time washing and waxing the car to impress her. He had clothing from home to change into before the date and used the station restroom to spruce up for the occasion.

It was a beautiful starlit night with a full moon. At 9:30 he pulled into the Marshall driveway. Walking to the porch he rang the bell. He smiled broadly as he turned to admire his new convertible with the top down sitting in the drive under the bright moonlight. The door opened an Eileen greeted him.

"Hi, Phil, how are you?" she asked.

"I'm good, and you?" he answered.

"I'm good," she replied. "Come on in, while I get my coat."

Stepping in to the living room, Eileen said to her parents. "Mom, Daddy, you remember Phil, don't you?"

"Oh, yes. Hello Phil," her father greeted him.

"Hi, Phil," her mother said, joining in the greeting.

"Hi folks. Nice to see you again," Phil responded.

Eileen took Phil's arm and asked, "Ready Phil?"

"Yes. Good night, folks. "Enjoy your evening," he said as they turned to leave.

"Seeing the car, Eileen asked, "Oh, Phil, is this your car?"

"U huh", he casually replied.

"Pat said you now had a car, but I didn't think it would be this nice. What kind is it?" she asked.

"A Cadillac," he answered, a little hurt she had not recognized the make of the car. I thought everybody knew what a Cadillac looked like, he reasoned.

"A Cadillac? I knew you were working, Phil, but I didn't realize you had struck it rich," she said jokingly.

That was one of the things Phil felt good about. Just because you had an expensive car everyone thought you were wealthy. To Phil, that was the wonderful thing about driving a prestigious car.

Their date ended up at a drive-in movie that evening and they did very little necking because of exposure in the convertible with the top down.

It was after midnight when Phil dropped off Eileen at her home. He wore a puzzled frown; he could not understand Eileen's demeanor. She seemed cold toward him. She had hardly responded when he kissed her. Unlike her usual self. Her lips were cold and without feeling.

"Is something wrong?" Phil asked.

"No, not a thing, Phil." She answered, giving no explanation for her unusual behavior toward him.

Phil got out of the car, opened the door for her, and they walked in silence to her door.

She refused a good night kiss with the lame excuse of, "The neighbors will see us."

He said good night, and walked back to the car. He sat for a few minutes while lighting a cigarette. He wondered again what the reason was, for her apparent coldness. Unable to find an answer he shrugged his shoulders, started the engine and, backed out of the driveway. He was disappointed with the entire evening.

Not ready to go home, he cruised the gut on Main Street. He suddenly thought of a cute little chick, who had been in the service station a couple of times since he had been working there.

He remembered her telling him she was the ex-wife of a serviceman who was now deployed overseas. He recalled with a grin how she wasn't bad to look at. Even though, he had not seen her figure. But if her figure matched her face, she would be a knock-out.

He tried to recall their conversation the last time she was in the station. He remembered they had talked about apartments. She shared she had just moved to a new luxury apartment house, closer to her work at the telephone company. He remembered she told him she worked shift work, but he didn't recall what days or hours. Didn't she give him her phone number? Or had he dreamed it? He pulled over, under a street light, and frantically searched his wallet. He recovered a small piece of paper tucked into the folding money compartment.

He wondered if she would be home in bed at this hour. Just for kicks, he found a phone booth. Dropping coins for a signal he dialed in the numbers. During the ringing he tried to remember her name. He thought was it either Debra or Sandra. When she answered, he decided he would call her Debra.

"Hello, Debra," he said.

"Hello. Who is this?" she asked.

"This is Phil. Phil Kingsley from the service station," he answered. "Maybe the name doesn't ring a bell to you, but you have been in to the service station where I work several times," he explained.

"Oh yes. I remember you. Where are you now at this hour?" she asked.

"I'm downtown," he replied.

"Are you drunk?" she asked

"No. I'm sorry to call so late, but I couldn't remember what hours or days you worked," he explained.

"I just got home an hour or so ago. I worked until 11:30, came home, showered, and went to bed," she said.

"I'm sorry I woke you up, but I'd like to see you", he said.

"Tonight?" she asked.

"No. Not tonight, unless you want to. But I'd like to have a date with you."

"Tonight?" she asked again.

"No. Not necessarily tonight, unless you want me to come over," he suggested.

"Are you crazy? It's past 1:30 in the morning," she exclaimed.

"Well, you don't have to see me right now. I just thought we could have coffee together and get acquainted," he explained.

"No. Not tonight. Maybe some other time," she said sleepily.

"Ok. Whenever you're in the area, drop in the station to see me," he invited.

"Alright. Good-bye," she replied.

"Good-bye" he said, before the line went dead. He realized he had done a stupid thing.

Suddenly, he was a very lonely person. Here he was with a fine car, a good paying job, with many friends and acquaintances. He was not unhappy, just very discontent. Something was missing, but he didn't know what. Oh well, he thought. What the hell? He had quite a few bucks in his pocket, so why not make a night of it?

He pulled into the parking lot of a brightly lit night club boldly announcing with a neon sign, "Cocktails, live music, dancing nightly." Unsure he would get served any drinks, but thinking it would be worth a try, he boldly entered the club. The dim lighting caused him to momentarily stop while his eyes adjusted to the semi-darkness. Walking to the bar he casually sat on a stool wanting to give the impression this behavior was an old pattern for him. The bartender moved down the bar and stopped in front of him.

"Yes Sir, what'll it be?" he asked.

"Beer," Phil replied.

"What kind?" the barkeeper asked.

"Draft," Phil ordered in an unnatural, gruff voice.

The bartender scrutinized Phil's face and asked, "Are you 21?"

"I've had the seven-year itch three times, if that's what you mean," Phil sarcastically retorted.

"Do you have any ID?" the bartender requested.

"Sure," Phil said. He reached for his wallet and pulled out a Press Card his boss Clay had loaned him, so he could get into local Sports events for free. Not knowing whether he could pull a bluff on the bartender, he decided to gamble it. Knowing he always looked older for his age he was counting on the dimness of the club to make him appear even older.

"How's this?" he asked placing the Press Card on the bar. The bartender picked it up, looked at it and handed it back. "It doesn't have your age, but I suppose it's alright; you look old enough. But you just can't be too careful," he said, as he set a schooner of beer in front of Phil. He declined the bill Phil pushed across the bar.

"Let this one be on the house. Maybe one of these days you can give us a little free publicity. I hope you were not offended by my asking for ID," he apologized.

"Naw. Forget it," Phil said waving off the encounter. The bartender left the conversation to wait on another customer.

Phil was thinking it worked. This joker really thought I'm a reporter. Boy, what a sucker. He even apologized for asking for ID thinking he might get a little free publicity. Wait until I tell Dave about this. We will have a good belly laugh.

Finishing the beer, he idly turned toward the sound of loud dance music playing in the background. The bartender was at his elbow in a matter of minutes with another schooner of beer. This time he accepted the crumpled bill Phil laid on the bar. Thanking the bartender, he again concentrated on the sound of music and the numbers of couples swinging, swaying bodies on the dance floor.

I gotta' remember this place he thought. It may be a good place to pick up a chick when I get desperate for a date. His dejected spirit had been lifted. He finished the beer and decided it was time to head for home. He noticed it was past two o'clock and the nightclub was getting ready to close when he waved good night to the bartender and left the club.

He decided he would make one last run through town before calling it a night. He cruised the length of Main Street, made a U turn and drove back in the direction from which he had just come. Driving through a yellow traffic light he did not see a pair of headlights flick on, from a side street, glide silently from the curb and pull in behind him. He cleared the city limits and picked up speed still unaware of the headlights following him from a distance.

He was thinking it had turned out to be as pretty good night, after all. His foot was heavy on the accelerator when the blinding red glare reflected in his rear-view mirror, and the scream of a Siren shattered his thoughts. He quickly signaled, pulled over, stopped, and killed the engine. A burley police officer with flashlight in hand appeared and stood beside his door.

"Good morning! Let me see your driver's license and registration," the officer requested.

Phil handed him his driver's license and said, "The registration is not in my name yet. I just bought the car."

"Take the license out of the folder, please. Do you know why I stopped you?' the officer asked.

"No. I don't," Phil replied.

"Well, you went through a yellow caution light at 39th Street, and you were going forty-seven miles per hour in a thirty-five mile per hour zone. You're out kinda' late, aren't you?" the officer asked.

"Yes. I am," Phil replied, "I'm just going home from taking my girl to a late movie," he said stretching the truth.

"I would suggest you go to earlier movies and be more careful when driving," the officer warned.

"I'll remember that," Phil replied.

"I won't ticket you for going through the yellow light, but I will cite you for speeding," he continued. He wrote out the ticket, and handed it to Phil to sign. Explaining that, signing the ticket was not an admission of guilt, rather, an acknowledgment that he was cited for speeding. "You will have to appear in municipal court two weeks from next Monday. The date and location of the court is written on the ticket." The officer stated. "Slow down, and be safe out there. Good night," he said before returning to the police car.

"Good night," Phil said returning the comment.

Boy! What a night it had been. First, he and Eileen didn't hit it off. Then Debra wouldn't see him, and now, a ticket for speeding. My luck is really changing, he thought to himself.

He wondered how much the ticket would cost. He had heard it was $2.00 for every mile over the speed limit. He quickly calculated; that was 12 miles over the speed limit, which meant, if his calculations were correct, he would get fined $24.00 dollars. Man! Over a half a week's salary!

On the way home he spoke out loud to himself, a quote he had heard many times from his dad, "When it rains, it pours". It sure is pouring on me. My luck is really down, he thought, feeling sorry for himself, he pulled into the driveway at home.

Things will have to get better, he promised himself. They sure can't get any worse, or so he thought.

CHAPTER 7

For Better or Worse

Phil was uneasy and troubled when he went to work on Sunday. His father was again ailing in health, and refusing to see a doctor. He also knew his mother would soon be giving birth to another sibling which would add more anxiety to her already stressful life.

Arriving at work he had a lot of time to think. Many people were out of town and business was slow. He was much concerned over what was going on in his life. He wondered what he would do after finishing high school. Would he go to college? He knew this would not be financially possible unless he was able to pay his own way, which didn't seem likely.

He pondered these weighty thoughts, always coming back to the same conclusion. He asked himself, why should I be concerned? I'm young, have a fairly good job, a nice car, and all my life ahead of me. Why am I plagued about the future? Why can't I be just like everyone else and take things as they come, one day at a time? Trying to push these thoughts from his mind, he busied himself with the radio trying to find some good sounding music. Hearing the alarm bell strip triggered, he was pleased when he recognized Dave's car pulling into the station.

"Hi Dave," he greeted his friend.

"Hey, Phil. How's tricks?" Dave asked.

"Man, I'm about to go nuts with nothing to do. Seems like everyone is out of town today."

"Well, that figures. Can't blame them. I'd be gone too for the weekend if Pat could have gone with me," Dave replied.

"Yeah. That's the only thing I don't like about this job. I have to work when everyone else is playin'", Phil said.

Changing the subject, Dave asked, "How was your date last night?"

"Do you really want to know, or do you want me to lie to ya?" Phil asked.

"That bad, huh? I thought you and Eileen got along real good."

"We did. But not last night. She seemed to be very cold. Just not the same," Phil explained.

"Pat tells me she's been seein' someone else. Some 'Holy Joe' she met in church," Dave said.

"Oh well, we were not goin' steady," Phil replied. "That's her choice."

"Yeah, but she should have told ya," Dave consoled

"I guess so, but she's not the only pebble on the beach," Phil replied. "Wait'll I tell you about what I did after I took her home," Phil said. "You'll bust a gut laughin'".

Phil shared the events of the previous night with Dave. They both laughed hysterically when he got to the part about the bartender accepting the Press Card as ID. Dave empathized with Phil when he told him about the speeding ticket.

"Say, Phil. You don't have to appear in court for two weeks. Let me see if my old man can get it fixed for you," Dave suggested.

Phil remembered Dave's father was one of the town's leading attorneys. He knew he probably had a lot of influence with the powers that be. Phil thought for a few minutes and knew it would not be right to play dirty politics and get the ticket "fixed". So, he rejected the idea saying, "No, Dave. I got what was comin' to me and I'll have to face the consequences. I appreciate your concern and for wantin' to help me. Thanks just the same."

"What a glutton you are for punishment. But if that's what you want, have it your way," Dave replied.

The subject changed and they discussed the latest movies, gossip, and other topics.

Dave stayed, until just before seven o'clock he announced, "I gotta go. I have a date with Pat."

Phil was left alone with his thoughts.

Many weeks passed with Phil continuing to feel sorry for himself believing everyone has rejected him. During this time, he dated several girls he met through the station. He even took out a few from high school who before had never even bothered to know he was alive. It just wasn't the same, he told himself.

He could not recapture the charming companionship he had known with Eileen. In fact, he was still painfully aware of Eileen's rejection. He didn't realize it at the time, but he must have been in love with her and felt despondent that she did not share his affection. Although it may have been "puppy love" it felt very real to him. The truth was, he was having a real "pity party."

During the weeks and months which followed, unknown to Phil, events were happening, that would change the course of his life.

After the Christmas and New Year's holidays, school had started again. He soon adjusted to the hum drum drudgery of living two lives; that of going to school and of working almost full time.

Arriving home one evening after work he was surprised to find the house quiet and empty. Walking in to the dining room he found a note on the table which read, "We are at the hospital with Mother. What do you want, a sister or brother?"

Recognizing the scrawl of his oldest sister, he was amused by her sense of humor even in a time of seriousness, such as this. The note didn't say which hospital, so he went to the kitchen, fixed a sandwich, and sat down in the dining room, munching on the sandwich, and washing it down with cold coffee.

About eleven o'clock, he heard a car pull into the yard and knew the family was home. They burst into the house, his sister in the lead. "It's a girl! It's a girl! We have a baby sister!" she gleefully announced.

"Wonderful!" Phil said. Turning to his father he asked, "What are we gonna name her?" He was momentarily shocked when he looked at his father's pale and gaunt features under the bright dining room light.

"Your mother wants to name her Sharon," the father replied.

"Sharon, Sharon", Phil repeated the name. He liked the sound.

To Phil, the weeks really seemed to fly by. It didn't seem like any time until his mother was back home assuming her usual role as homemaker, wife, and mother. Except for baby Sharon's occasional crying nothing had changed.

Before he realized it, Phil was up to his neck preparing for final exams prior to the end of the school year. The stress of studying and working had begun to tell on him. He was losing weight and seemed to be tired all the time, never seeming to get enough rest and sleep. It was the end of June by the time his rapid pace of living slowed and he was more or less back to normal.

At the same time, without warning, his father had his most serious attack, of what he liked to call "rheumatism". He sat in a reclining chair in the living room wrapped in blankets, shaking uncontrollably, experiencing chills, and fever, complaining of being cold. In an attempt to escape the discomfort, which had taken over his body, he became an extremely heavy drinker consuming large quantities of liquor.

He would sit in a drunken stupor and daze, not saying anything to anyone. During one of his more lucid moments Phil's mother in desperation convinced him he needed to see a doctor the next day. When morning came, he felt a little better and argued that he was "going to be alright."

Despite his improvement, his wife persuaded him to keep the doctor appointment. Without further insistence he strode from the house and drove off to town to see the doctor.

In the meantime, Mrs. Kingsley called the family physician, Dr. Anderson. She asked the doctor to call as soon as her husband left the office to explain her husband's diagnosis. Dr. Anderson promised he would.

It was two hours later when the telephone on the hallway table rang. Running to answer she picked up the receiver and said, "Hello."

"May I speak to Mrs. Kingsley, please?" the voice requested.

"This is Mrs. Kingsley," she answered.

"Mrs. Kingsley. This is Dr. Anderson. You wanted me to call, concerning your husband's Diagnosis?"

"Yes. Yes doctor. What is the diagnosis?" she asked.

"I don't like to tell you this, but your husband is a very sick man. He is an acute alcoholic. I have advised him to immediately submit himself to a rehabilitation center, and to stop drinking."

"Is there a rehabilitation center you would recommend, doctor?" she asked.

"Yes. There is a very effective rehabilitation center located not far from your home. It's called Miracle Haven Recovery Center. They specialize in recovery of those who drink," the doctor gently said.

Mrs. Kingsley knew he was being kind to her and not using the term alcoholic. "Good, Doctor. Will you call and make arrangements?" she asked. "I will see that he gets there."

"Yes. I will." He promised, and then, since he was the family doctor asked, "How's baby Sharon?"

"She's fine, Doctor. Thanks for asking," she replied.

"Wonderful. Well, I'll see you for your next appointment. Bye for now."

"Thank you, Doctor. Good bye,"

"Oh, God," she murmured. "Please don't let anything serious happen, and please let Verle agree to get treatment," she pleaded with God.

Going to the kitchen she began preparing dinner. She was humming a gospel hymn when she heard a car come up the driveway. Going to the window she looked out to see her husband coming up the sidewalk from the garage. His step was light and head held high.

"Hello Verle, what did you find out?" she asked, already knowing the answer.

"Oh, just the usual. I have a germ that needs killing and I plan to do that right now. I'm gonna' drown it," he said reaching for a bottle he kept hidden in the cupboard. He lifted the bottle to his lips and took a long drink.

"Is that all?" she asked.

"Yeah, that's all," he said, grinning, and playfully slapping her on the backside.

"Now Verle, cut that out," she said. He laughed heartily, taking another drink from the bottle.

"Verle, I have never said much about your drinking, but you are slowly killing yourself," she said.

"Whatya' mean, killin' myself?" he asked.

"I spoke to Dr. Anderson, Verle. He told me he recommended you check into a rehabilitation center for treatment, and to stop drinking," she explained.

"What? Of goin' to a rehabilitation center to be treated like a prisoner? No way! Not me! I ain't goin' nowhere, except back to work tomorrow," he exclaimed with a sharp tone.

"Verle. The doctor said you were a very sick man. I will not stand by and see you drive yourself to an early grave. I have asked him to make arrangements for you to be admitted at Miracle Haven Recovery Center for you to go and have rest and care," she said sternly.

"Ya' had no business doin' that. I'm not a kid. I could have made arrangements myself," he said defiantly.

"Verle, whether you like it or not, you owe it to me, the kids, and yourself to get professional help. If you don't go, I'll be forced to take the children and leave you," she said giving him an ultimatum. She was surprised at her burst of anger. It was the first time in thirty years of marriage she had ever used the threat of breaking up their marriage to achieve her purpose. Her husband was startled at the convincing and definite tone of voice.

"Ok, ok. We'll see," he replied and left the room.

When Phil came home that evening, she told him, in whispers, of his father's serious condition and the plan to admit him to a rehabilitation center.

Bright and early the next morning, Phil went with his parents to the rehabilitation center for the father's admission, and presumed stay, on the long road to recovery. It was noon before Verle Kingsley was admitted, and assigned a room. Phil and his mother said good bye, with the assurance they would visit on the weekend, and left the facility.

Verle unpacked the suitcase. He slyly grinned, when he took three bottles of 100 proof "white lightnin" from the bag, and slipped them under the mattress.

On the weekends he always seemed to be in a cheerful mood when the family visited, and was seemingly responding to treatment. Phil learned from his mother, who had spoken to the doctor, that Verle had not expressed any desire for alcohol, so far. Her happiness bubbled over when she told him, "If he continues to improve, he could soon be discharged from the rehabilitation center and come home."

They were not aware he had sneaked alcohol into the rehabilitation center, and during the past six weeks, had also been receiving additional alcohol from a so-called friend.

CHAPTER 8

Tragedy – Death Takes its Toll

The seventh week of his father's residency at the rehabilitation center Phil was working and had just finished changing oil and lubricating a customer's car.

The customer had hung around the station watching him work and swapping jokes with him. By the time he finished, and the customer left, it was almost closing time.

Phil started pulling the oil and tire rack displays from the gas pump islands, rolling them inside the garage. He pushed the lever to close the overhead garages door, and watched while they noisily closed. No sooner had the door closed when he heard the telephone ringing. He debated whether to answer, since it was now past closing. Letting good business practice win the debate, he picked up the receiver.

"Clay's Service. How can I help you?" he answered.

"Phil? Phil?" a tearful voice questioned.

Recognizing his mother's voice, he said, "Yes. This is Phil."

"Phil, something terrible has happened. Can you come home right away?"

"Yes. What's happened? What's wrong?" he asked.

"I'll tell you when you get home. Hurry," she answered sobbing.

"Ok Mom. I'm closing the station right now. I'll be there as soon as I can," he assured her.

He could not imagine what had happened to make his mother's voice, usually so soft and controlled, sound so high pitched, troubled, and unnatural.

He hurriedly finished closing chores, and locked the main front door. Removing the money from the register he placed it in the floor safe, before turning out the lights. He unlocked the door, and walked out, locking the door behind him. He stepped out into the coolness of the night and quickly walked to his car.

Every light in the house was on when he arrived home and pulled into the driveway. Leaving the car, he ran the short distance to the house. Inside he could hear sobbing voices and could see his mother and oldest sister embracing and crying uncontrollably. A younger sister ran to him placing her arms around him. "Oh, Phil, something awful has happened," she said between sobs.

"Try to control yourself, and tell me what has happened?" he gently demanded.

"Daddy's dead," she answered, still sobbing.

"Dead? How? When?'" he asked, moving toward his mother, attempting to comfort her.

"They don't know for sure, Son. They are going to do an autopsy," she answered with a broken voice.

"How did it happen, Mom?" Phil asked, trying to make sense of it.

"There was a police car waiting here when we came home from prayer meeting. That was just a little while before I called you," she explained. "They told us your father had left the rehabilitation center with a friend and gone downtown to a bar. They started drinking heavily, and got drunk. They decided to go to a restaurant to eat. They ordered a big dinner, but when the food was served, your father barely touched his, and Complianed of a headache."

"They decided to do some more drinking and walked toward the car. Before reaching the car, your father stumbled, lost his balance and fell, striking his head on the pavement. An ambulance was called, but they were not able to resuscitate him. They don't know the cause of his death. They suspect a massive heart attack from the fall. The coroner says they will have to perform an autopsy."

"Oh, Phil!! What are we going to do?" she asked, through a fresh surge of tears.

Phil searched his memory for Scripture that would be comforting. Try as he might, he could not think of a single verse.

Suddenly, he did remember a verse, he heard quoted many times in church, from the book of Romans, Chapter 8, and verse 28. Embracing his mother, he quoted as much as he could remember; "… Mom, the Bible says, all things work together for good, to those who love the Lord…." Trying to convince himself more than his mother. He wondered what good could come from his father's death.

"I know, Son. It's so good of you to comfort me with the Word of God. You're such a good son," she said quietly.

Phil knew his mother would not have this opinion of him if she could read his thoughts. Why had God permitted this to happen?" He recalled another verse promising. "…ask and you will receive…" Hadn't he asked God to cure his father for his mother's sake? He was bitter toward God for not receiving what he had prayed for. He was uncertain his prayers ever reached beyond the ceiling. The more he thought about his prayers not being answered, the more angry and bitter he became. He visualized himself shaking his fist in God's face saying, "I don't need you, God. I'll get along without you."

The coroner's report from the autopsy was no surprise to the family. It read, "Cause of Death: Acute intracranial hematoma; cerebral hemorrhage, related to fall, resulting in cardiac arrest"

Following the untimely death of Verle Kingsley, the funeral memorial service was scheduled for the middle of the week on a Wednesday. Phil with the family arrived at the mortuary and were silently escorted into the chapel.

Phil, who at times, hated his father sat next to his mother unmoved. While the death of his father had erased any animosity, he was dry-eyed. The organ music stopped and the family pastor presented the eulogy. Phil silently prayed he could cry, so that he would not be the only dry-eyed family member.

The eulogy ended, the casket was opened and the procession began passing by family members and bier, offering condolences and paying final respects. Phil was glad to feel tears sliding down his cheeks.

The procession over, they walked to the parking lot and entered the family car parked behind the coach. It seemed to Phil an eternity before reaching the cemetery to witness the pastor reading the 23rd Psalm, ending by saying, "*Earth to earth, ashes to ashes, and dust to dust,*" before blessing the people. The casket was lowered into the freshly dug grave.

A decision had been made by the family to not have a reception, following the funeral memorial service. Watching the long line of slow-moving cars exit the cemetery, Phil impatiently waited for the family car to take them home.

Many thoughts raced through Phil's mind driving home. What were they going to do? Would he have to quit school to help support the family? He felt no elation at the unwanted position of head of the family. He was unlearned in the way the state and federal governments cared for families of deceased. It was only a very short time until the family was receiving aid for dependent children under the age of eighteen, and a Social Security check to his mother as surviving spouse of his late father.

A week after losing his father, school started again. Many of his classmates and friends stopped him in the hallway to offer condolences. With each expression of sympathy Phil became increasingly bitter over the death of his father and with God for letting him die. By the time he returned to work he was so completely angry and frustrated his bitterness had turned to hate.

He was feeling sorry for himself when he recognized Debra, the telephone operator, driving into the station, stopping at the pumps. He was so glad to see someone who knew little or nothing about him that he almost shouted. Quickly moving to her car, he greeted her, "Hi, Debra. How are you?" he asked. Not waiting for her reply, he continued, "Gee. It's been a long time since I have seen you."

"Hi Phil. I'm good. And you?" she asked.

"I'm ok", he replied and asked, "Do you need gas?"

"No. I wanted to come by and apologize for my attitude, and behavior the time you called," she explained.

"Aw, you don't have to apologize. It was stupid of me to call you at that hour," he replied.

"Well, anyway, I also wanted to ask, what you are doing this evening?" she asked.

"I don't have any plans. Why do you ask?" he inquired.

"I thought I would take you up on that get-acquainted cup of coffee," she replied

"Great. What time and where shall I meet you?" he asked.

"I don't feel like going out, so why don't you come by my apartment?" she invited.

"Perfect. What's the address?" he asked.

She scribbled her address and apartment number on a note pad, tore off the page, and handed it to him.

"Squire Arms," he read looking at the name of the apartment house. "You're really living in style," he said with a smile.

"No. Not really, but it's nice," she replied.

"Super, Debra. I'll see you tonight, but I don't get off until nine; it will be after that. Is that ok?" he asked.

"Sure. I don't have to work tomorrow," she replied.

"Good. I'll see you then," he said.

"Got it. Just ring my bell. Bye, bye," she said, and drove out of the station.

Pleased he had a date, he suddenly realized he better call his mother and tell her he would be late coming home so she wouldn't worry.

Pulling up in front of the Squire Arms apartments building, he was met by a uniformed doorman, who took keys to the car, and gave him an identification claim check. He walked in to the plush carpeted foyer. Pausing at the resident directory he noted a Debra Drake – Apartment 312. Punching the button beside the name, a female voice asked, "Who is it?"

"It's Phil, Debra," he answered.

"Come on up, Phil," she invited. Crossing the lobby, he went to the bank of elevators,

Pushing the call button for the 3rd floor he waited. Stepping into the elevator, and exited on the 3rd floor.

Looking at the directional arrows, he turned right and stopped in front of Apartment 312 and rang the bell.

"A soft voice enquired," Who is it?"

Placing his mouth close to the door, he replied, "It's Phil, Debra."

He heard the sound of a bolt being released, and the door opened.

"Hi, Phil, you made it. Come on in," she invited.

"Hi, yourself," he said. Stepping into the dimly lighted apartment. He noticed she was wearing only a silk night gown, with a robe carelessly tossed around her shoulders. His suspicions were confirmed about her body, matching her face. The sheer night gown revealed the fullness of her breasts.

He followed her across the thick carpet to the sofa. She invited him to sit. Feeling self-conscious he reached for a cigarette. Pulling out a pack of king size he took out two, lit them and handed one to Debra.

The scent of expensive perfume mingled with the smell of alcohol touched his nostrils as she reached out to accept the lighted cigarette. The unsteadiness of her hand, coupled with the alcoholic breath led Phil to think she had been drinking heavily.

"What would you like? Scotch or Bourbon?" she asked.

"Scotch, straight," he replied, hoping he would like it.

Disappearing into the kitchenette she soon returned with two glasses and a decanter of Scotch. Lifting the cap on the decanter she generously poured the Scotch into each glass. "What do you want for a chaser," she asked.

"Water will be fine," he answered. Going again to the kitchenette she returned with two more glasses and a pitcher of ice water.

"A toast", she offered. "A toast to our first date. May we have a good time," she said, touching her raised glass to his, and taking a sip of Scotch.

Going to the hi-fi record player she set a stack of long-play records spinning. Phil appreciated her musical taste when he recognized a selection from the album called "Dinner for Two."

Straightening up from the hi-fi, she turned toward the French windows. Moving noiselessly across the plush rug she opened them wide. Twin shafts of moonlight streamed in, to lie shimmering on the carpet.

Debra joined him on the sofa. They toasted again "To Friendship." Phil, starting to feel good from a second drink, suggested they dance on the balcony to the sound of the now playing "Stardust."

Gliding into his arms they warmly embraced and danced several selections cheek to cheek. Holding her tightly in his arms, he noticed her cheek was hot, and her face was flushed.

Tiring of dancing, they retraced their steps to the sofa. Sitting side by side, breath slightly stimulated from the exercise of alcohol and dancing.

Debra's hands slid under Phil's shirt and up his back, with the other hand running through his hair. Alcoholic courage caused him to slip his arms around her, gently pulling her toward him. Their lips met. Lightly at first. Then eagerly. Phil felt her tongue slip between his lips seeking his tongue. They hungrily kissed, kindling their passion.

Debra suddenly broke from their embrace exclaiming, "I need a drink!"

"So do I," he said, and poured two more drinks from the decanter. His hand was trembling when he offered the drink to her.

After refreshing their drinks Phil turned over the stack of long-play records on the hi-fi player and lit each of them a cigarette. They smoked in silence; the sound of music again filled the room. Their cigarettes were only half-smoked, when Phil lifted Debra's from her hand, and stubbed both his and hers out in the ashtray.

He took her in his arms and begin kissing her neck, forehead, and ears. Her breath quickened as she ran the tip of her tongue behind his ear, and down his neck.

Suddenly Phil could no longer stand the uncontrollable passion. He sought her lips, pressing his body tightly to her. Their lips met again. The tip of her tongue ran through his lips eagerly moving back and forth. He responded by caressing her bare breasts under the sheer negligee.

Unable to calm his raging passion, he lifted and carried her to the bedroom, placing her on the bed. Hurriedly undressing, he lay beside her. Their lips met again. The distance between them closed. Sounds of ecstasy and pleasure escaped her throat when he seduced her.

CHAPTER 9

Anxiety, Frustration, and Unrest

The pattern of Phil's extra-curricular activities was beginning to take its toll; his school grades were plummeting. He was being repeatedly called into the Dean's office for being on low grade reports. He had become anxious, frustrated, and disgusted with school. He was seriously thinking about dropping out, and quitting school. To bring his grades back up, he would have to do some extra studying which he was not interested in doing.

The passing of his father had obligated him to provide transportation for the family on Sunday to and from church. He disliked it intensely, but had no choice in the matter. He hated it for several reasons. One, it cut into his work schedule, reducing his salary. Two, he was now living a life in direct conflict with church character. He lived in constant anxiety and frustration, torn between two opposite and very different life styles; that which was expected of him, as a church goer, and that which he had a desire to live.

He had long ago stopped calling his mother to tell her he was going to be late; he was invariably late.

One Saturday night the church was sponsoring a well-known guest, a youth speaker. Although his mother was not going, she insisted he attend. Promising he would, he immediately resented it. To console himself he stopped off after work at a local pub to have a few beers so he could "enjoy" himself at the meeting. Not wanting to be late, he bought a six-pack of beer to take along with him, knowing he would have opportunity to sneak out to his car, and have a "quickie" drink.

He arrived in time to join in refreshment time, and enjoyed eating bite size sandwiches, and drinking some fruit punch. Deciding this was too mild for him, he sneaked out a back door and strode to his car. He had just finished drinking a beer when a figure walked around the side of his car. The figure turned when he saw someone in the car and came over to say hello. It was Reverend Boris. Phil froze. He didn't know what to do with the beer can he held. The reverend approached the car and recognized Phil.

"Good evening, Phil. Why aren't you inside with the others enjoying yourself?" he asked, stopping by the side of the car.

"I just stepped out for a breath of fresh air," Phil replied, hoping to bluff his way out of an embarrassing situation.

The reverend sniffed, recognizing the smell of alcohol. "Are you drinking, Phil?" he asked.

"Yes. As a matter of fact, I am," he answered.

"You would break your mother's heart, if she knew of this," the reverend admonished him.

"Yeah. I know I shouldn't be doing it," Phil admitted. "But ya' know the old sayin', 'Like father, like son'," he continued.

"You know that's not true, Phil. A man can be what he wants to be, with God's help," the reverend replied.

"I hope you don't say anything to my mother. It would only add to her burden of worry," Phil pleaded with the Rev.

"Rely on me not to tell her Son, but just know, I'm going to be praying for you," the reverend assured him.

"Thanks Reverend," Phil said, as he started the engine and pulled from the parking lot.

A half mile from the church he pulled over and opened another can of beer. He drained the last sip of beer from the can and reached for another. Finishing that beer, he lit a cigarette and smoked.

A few minutes later he decided it was no fun drinking alone. Crushing out the half-smoked cigarette in the ashtray, he reached for the starter. He decided to call Debra to see if she was home. He pulled into a service station, and parked in front of a public phone booth. Depositing a coin, he dialed her number and impatiently waited for the connection. The phone rang incessantly.

He decided to call the telephone company to see if Debra was working. Depositing another coin, he dialed the operator. Requesting the phone company number, he asked the operator to connect him. A pleasant, but monotonous voice answered the call. "Good evening, Northeastern Telephone. How may I help you?"

"Yes, please connect me with the Personnel Supervisor," Phil requested.

"After a few minutes of silence, a crisp, clear voice spoke, "Personnel Supervisor, Mary speaking. Go ahead please. How may I help you?"

"Hello, I would like some information on one of your employees," Phil said.

"I'm sorry, Sir. Information on our employees is confidential," the supervisor replied.

"I'm not asking for personal information. She is family," Phil lied, "I just want to know if she is working tonight. Can you tell me what shift Ms. Debra Drake is working?" he insisted.

"Just a moment, please. Let me check", the supervisor replied. After a minute or two of silence, the supervisor responded. "Sir, in reply to your request, Ms. Drake is scheduled to work the three o'clock to 11:30 shift today."

"Thank you very much, Ma'am," Phil replied.

Over the receiver, he heard the operator say, "That will be another fifty-cents. Please deposit." He deposited the coins. It was worth the small price. He was pleased with himself that he played detective to obtain the information, even if he had to tell a white lie to get it.

He wondered, should he meet her after work at the telephone company or should he meet her at the apartment house? Deciding on the latter, he recalled he had not seen her for several weeks and he did not know what her attitude would be at him casually dropping in unannounced.

Entering the apartment building he walked to the lobby and choose a chair in view of the main entrance. Hiding his face behind a newspaper, he sat down to wait. Shortly before midnight he heard her now familiar voice greeting the doormen who held the door for her entrance.

He waited until she crossed the lobby, and entered the elevator. Before tossing the paper aside, he nervously puffed on a cigarette and impatiently waited five minutes before walking to the elevator. He punched the 3rd floor button and silently prayed Debra would not be angry with him, and she would be pleased to see him.

The elevator stopped, the doors silently sliding open. Leaving the elevator, he walked to her apartment number and rang the bell pausing with his ear close to the door. Hearing no sound, he softly tapped. Several minutes passed before he heard a voice asking, "Who is it?"

"It's Phil, Baby. Can I come in?" he invited himself.

As before, he heard the sliding back of a dead bolt, and then the door opened.

"Why Phil! What a nice surprise!" she exclaimed. "Sorry it took so long to answer. I was getting ready to take a shower," she explained.

Phil waited for a moment, not knowing if it was pleasure, or sarcasm edging her voice.

"I'm sorry I didn't call you, but I had to see you," he explained.

"It's just as well you didn't call. I wouldn't have been home. I was working; I just got home."

Oh, good," he said, trying to show surprise, "Then I didn't get you out of bed."

"Well, come on in, unless you want to entertain the neighbors," she jokingly said. "Why don't you fix us a drink? Everything is in the refrigerator. I'm going to shower".

"Ok, call me when you finish, I'll towel you off," Phil playfully replied.

"Thanks a bunch," she said leaving for the bathroom, and a shower.

In the kitchenette he found a decanter of Scotch. Taking two glasses from the cabinet, he carried them and the decanter to the living room, sitting them on the glass-topped coffee table. Removing the top, he turned the mouth of the decanter over each glass pouring generously. Using tongs, he lifted ice cubes from a bucket, and placed the cubes in each glass. He was sipping a drink, and smoking a cigarette, when Debra, clad only in a sheer negligée, joined him.

The rise and fall of her bosom pressing against the ties, forced the negligee open, revealing the fullness of her breasts.

Sitting down beside Phil, she lifted her glass, and drank thirstily of the Scotch as though it was water.

She ran her fingers through his hair, placed her face close to his, seeking his lips, running her tongue in and out of his mouth. Phil soon thought, it was the same pattern as before. He wondered if he was the only guy she was seeing? After sex, he was disappointed with himself, and disapproving of Debra, because she was so driven by uncontrollable passion, and was so easy to seduce.

Having dated many women since last seeing Debra, he was disapproving of her, for the lack of controlled resistance many females offered, at first. He was disappointed with himself, because the challenge of conquest was removed. He missed the thrill of rising passion, and the persuasion to win them over, with rising, uncontrolled emotions, and flaming passion, giving a sense of victory,

Weeks and months passed. His experience had been only a prelude to the life Phil had now come to accept as common place. His school grades continued to suffer while he wined and dined his now many female acquaintances. His small savings dwindled. He found it difficult to meet his car payment, and to pay his mother room and board.

Every day he made up his mind to quit school and to get a better full-time job. Still, he continued to attend as though he had fallen into a rut. In truth, he didn't have the courage to break his ties and launch out into an entirely new environment of uncertainty.

He need not have been worried. The decision had abruptly been made for him, as he was soon to learn. One day arriving at work, the usual "hellos" were exchanged. But something was different. Clay was acting peculiar. He approached Phil and said, "I don't like to have to tell you this, but I'm selling the station."

"Why?" Phil asked, surprised. "You're not going broke, are you?"

"No. You remember me telling you my wife's mother had a heart attack? Well, she's not expected to live. My wife wants us to go back East and be with her for as long as she lives, and to take care of her aging father." Clay explained.

"I'm sorry to learn that, Clay. But I know you wanna' do what's right," Phil said, empathizing with Clay.

"I don't know if the fella buying the station will need you, Phil. He has two grown sons who'll run the garage, and he plans to run the station himself," Clay explained.

"Well, that's the breaks," Phil remarked, trying to be accepting. "I sure wanna' thank you, Clay, for giving me a job, and putting up with me for as long as you have."

"I was glad to help you out." Clay replied, and continued. "It'll take a couple of weeks before we get things settled, and the new owner takes over. So, let's don't get the cart in front of the horse." Clay remarked, said good night to Phil and walked to his car.

Phil was thinking out loud, "Well, that's a fine kettle of fish. I've been worrying about what to do about school, and the decision has suddenly been made for me."

Phil didn't have any idea what kind of job he would look for. The only thing he had experience with was at the service station, and he doubted he could find a full-time station attendant job, because most stations in the area were family owned and staffed.

His mind was made up. He said to himself, "I will definitely have to quit school, unless I can find a part-time job that won't conflict with school hours, which will also enough to pay my car payment, board and room, and lifestyle," he rationalized.

CHAPTER 10

A New Vocation

Phil searched the employment ads every day, and applied for several that seemed promising, but had not been able to meet the qualifications for employment.

One day, he noticed an advertisement that was of particular interest. It read:

WANTED

"Ambitious young man
To train as Ambulance Driver."

The rest of the ad was lost on him, as he hurriedly ran to the phone, and asked to speak to the supervisor in charge of the advertisement.

He was able to schedule an appointment interview for the next morning at ten o'clock. He knew he would have to skip school in order to keep the appointment; nothing could have bothered him less.

Arriving at the ambulance agency he scored a successful interview, lied about his age, and was employed as an Ambulance Driver Trainee. He was oblivious to the fact this job was to impact the path of his future.

On the first assignment, an emergency call, the supervisor drove, starting to teach him the basic fundamentals of ambulance driving. He explained the various actions behind the wheel.

"You notice this is a very narrow road with narrow shoulders. So, you want to use the siren a lot along with the flashing red and blue lights. Run the siren up and down; let it run for a full scream and then, let it run down to a groan, while blasting on the horn. This lets the oncoming drivers hear it, as well as the traffic you are passing. If you let the siren scream at its full pitch, at your excessive speed, all the sound would go behind you," the supervisor explained to him.

Phil nodded his understanding, and remarked in a complimentary voice. "That's a very good point."

"Another thing. When you receive a call for an ambulance, always ask, 'Is this an emergency?'. The police watch us very closely, on our operation, and sometimes follow us to our destination, as we break speed limits, and demand right-of-way, to make sure the call is an emergency, and not a joy-ride", the supervisor explained. At another time, Phil was to learn this first hand.

Traveling at speeds in excess of 90 miles an hour, they soon reached their destination. Slowing the ambulance, the supervisor checked addresses; finding the correct one, he braked to a stop, and with the siren growling, backed the ambulance into a long driveway. Phil noticed when he parked the ambulance, he left the engine running.

Before exiting the ambulance, the supervisor said, "This is another very important point, Phil. Always leave the engine running after a run. The flashing lights and siren pull a lot of juice, and if you shut off the motor, you might not be able to get it started," he explained.

Together, they got out of the ambulance and walked to the rear. Opening the wide doors, they removed the gurney and wheeled it to the patient's door. The door opened; a gray-haired, worried looking man urged them to "Please hurry!"

Moving the gurney to the side of the patient's bed, the supervisor taught Phil how to lift, and transfer, the patient from the bed to the gurney. The patient grimaced in pain when transferred cautioning them to "Be careful of my hip' I think it's broken." The husband hurriedly told the ambulance attendants details about his wife's accident, as they wheeled the gurney to the ambulance placing it inside and locking it in place.

"She was standing on a step-ladder washing windows, when the ladder toppled and she fell", he explained.

"Sir, are you going to follow us to General Hospital?" Supervisor Carl asked.

"Yes. I am," the husband replied.

"We will be admitting her through the ambulance entrance to the emergency room, Sir. You will need to go to the emergency room when you arrive, and explain what happened," the supervisor explained.

Turning to Phil he said, "Phil, you ride in back with the patient. Due to the serious condition of the patient, we will be making an Emergency run to the Hospital," he explained.

Turning on flashing red and blue lights, the ambulance exited the driveway, and entered the freeway on-ramp with the siren screaming. Arriving at the hospital they quickly pulled into a zone marked "Ambulance Only."

In the days following, Phil learned in detail the ambulance business. For instance, that you should never speed through a red light, but slow down to twenty-five miles an hour to avoid a collision; that you should not accept a police escort, which was surprising to him. But Supervisor Carl, explained, "If the escort, with siren and flashing lights runs through an intersection against a red light, traffic may assume, the police car was the only emergency vehicle and start up, causing an accident with the ambulance."

"That makes common sense," Phil commented, he was glad Carl explained it to him.

The second call with Supervisor Carl was to an accident where a teen-ager had been hit riding a bicycle. Emergency calls came fast and often. After about the sixth call he lost count. He did remember a call to a mother who was in premature labor; and the heart patient who was

DOA (Dead on Arrival) at the hospital, and the female patient who had sustained as compound-fracture resulting from a fall. And many, many more emergency calls to service.

Supervisor Carl, satisfied Phil had learned well as a trainee, released him to be a "journeyman driver." He was then introduced to an older member of the family owned ambulance business named Mel, who no longer felt safe as an ambulance driver, but wanted to stay active as an assistant. Since each ambulance had a crew of two attendants, a driver and assistant, Phil and Mel became partners. He and Mel were dispatched to an accident still fresh in Phil's mind.

They received an emergency call from the State Highway Patrol requesting them to proceed to the scene of an accident with injuries, approximately 10 miles from their office. Driving at excessive speed, with siren screaming on Highway I-5 Phil experienced a very close call.

Driving over a hill on a two-lane highway at eighty miles an hour, he was rolling downhill toward a bridge built for expansion to four lanes. The two extra lanes had been completed, but had not yet been opened, and remained a two-lane bridge across the river. The unopened lanes were cordoned off with raised, parallel six-inch pavement risers, until a construction crew could stripe the two new lanes.

Approaching the bridge, Phil's heart began racing, and his throat tightened, when he saw a vehicle passing cars in his lane, headed toward him. The distance was fast closing between him and the oncoming vehicle. It appeared the driver was unmindful of the flashing red and blue lights and sound of the siren. Panic set in when Phil glanced at the speedometer and realized he had slowed down by only ten miles per hour due to inertia and the heavy weight of the ambulance. He frantically fastened his eyes on the oncoming car, wondering, as he was approaching the bridge, how to avoid a head-on collision with the car in his lane, still coming toward him,

He was afraid if he pulled across the pavement risers, he would lose control of the ambulance and crash into the side of the bridge on into the stream of oncoming traffic. His thoughts racing, he spun the steering wheel of the ambulance over the raised dividers into the unopened lanes of the bridge. There was a resounding thud when the tires struck the raised dividers, when he and the car occupying his lane passed with only inches to spare avoiding a head-on accident. He gripped the steering wheel tightly. The ambulance traveled approximately 150 feet, see-sawing in his grasp attempting to go out of control, before again reaching smooth pavement.

Frightfully shaken, and sweating profusely, he fought to gain composure and stomped the accelerator to the floor, putting pedal to metal, attempting to make up for lost time.

Mel complimented Phil on his driving, "Great job, Phil. I thought we were goners!"

Approaching the accident, it was obvious what had happened. A car had collided head-on with a pick-up truck attempting to pass an eighteen-wheel tractor trailer. With a pile-up of cars behind the car hit, there were multiple injuries.

Another ambulance and two tow trucks were at the scene when Phil and Mel arrived. A State Highway Patrol Officer instructed them to remove the female driver of the car, who appeared to be unconscious. Quickly examining the patient for broken bones, and finding none, they removed her from the wrecked car placing her on a gurney and transferred to the ambulance, locking the gurney in place.

Mel entered the ambulance, and sat down next to the patient. Phil still nervous from the near head-on collision eased the ambulance away from the accident, activated the flashing red and blue lights, turned on the siren and soon was speeding down the highway, headed for the nearest city and hospital. The siren sounded in the stillness of the night, repeatedly rose to a crescendo, and fading to an uneven monotone.

Regaining consciousness, the patient groaned, and stirred enroute to the hospital. She complained of back pain, and of being cold. Mel pulled a blanket from a storage box and tucked it around her. He then reached for the switch to the heater occupying the lower half of the 02 (oxygen) equipment compartment. In a matter of minutes, the heat blasting from the heater removed the chill inside the ambulance.

The patient, although in pain, wanted to talk. "What do you think is wrong with my back?" she asked Mel.

"I don't know, Ma'am. I'm not medical," he said.

"But you've been around a lot of people with back injuries, haven't you?" she questioned.

"As I said, I don't know. It could be a fractured spine," he replied.

"That's very serious," she said in a troubled voice, almost to herself.

"Yes, Ma'am. That would be serious. Although, it may only be a severe sprain," he said, and continued, "I'm not diagnosing, Ma'am. As I said, I'm not medical."

"Let's pray that's all it is," she invited his prayers.

During the drive to the hospital she explained her husband was a retired pastor. She enquired about his safety. How is my husband? Is he coming to the hospital?" she asked.

"As far as I know, you were the only one in your car that was injured," Mel told her.

"Oh, thank God," she answered.

Speeding through the blackness of the night she gazed out the window and called Mel's attention to a billboard posted in the interest of those facing Spiritual warfare. It read, "The wages of sin is death; the gift of God is Eternal Life." Turning to Mel, in her state of semi-shock, she asked, "Are you a Christian, Sir?"

"Well... I, uh... have a religious background," he replied.

"Oh, how wonderful! You must have excellent opportunities to witness for Christ in your line of work. Being able to minister to those who are both physically and spiritual needy," she continued.

Mel was embarrassed not knowing how to answer, he remained silent.

"How many souls have you led to Christ?" she asked.

"None that I know of," he answered. He wondered how she could be so concerned over these issues when she was in pain from a possible severe injury. Mel was very uncomfortable in her presence by the time they reached the hospital.

The Highway Patrol had told the husband what hospital the ambulance was taking his wife to. He arrived shortly after the ambulance. He met them in the emergency room, where she was turned over to the competent care of the emergency room doctor and nurses.

She would not let Mel go until she had the address of the ambulance company in order to inform him of her recovery.

Weeks later she wrote Mel and "That other nice young man," a card thanking them for their kind, caring service, letting them know she had only suffered a severe sprain to her back, and informed them she "will be praying for each of you."

Mel shared the card and information with Phil, who was deeply touched, amazed that a Higher Power, God as he would come to know Him, was trying to get his attention.

CHAPTER 11

The Last Word

The nerve-racking emergency calls and stress of strenuous broken hours of sleep began to take their toll on Phil. After one particular "close call," driving on a heavily congested highway, he returned to the ambulance office quarters, and reflected on the serious chances he had to take, in order to meet the obligation requirement of the job. He would smoke heavily, and on days off, would drink to the point of being drunk. Considering the risks of the job, he found himself literally shaking with delayed nervous reaction.

In desperation, trying to forget the risk taking, the drinking became excessive, and his time off was consumed by the wrong kind of female company. His mind was ill at ease; torn between two conflicting factors; trying to do what was right, and continuing to do, what he knew to be wrong. He was oblivious to a huge transition occurring in his young life.

First, maturing from late childhood to manhood, and second, a desire to change from having low morals and what he believed to be a rejected lifestyle, to the reality of a Spiritual awakening. His life would soon sink to a new low.

One late afternoon, in a foul mood, Phil returned to work from having a day off. He had been stood up by one of his latest female acquaintances; his anger was heated by alcohol. He pulled into and parked in an area next to the attendant living quarters. He noticed Supervisor

Carl critically eyeing the ambulance sitting in the open double garage. He called to Phil as he approached.

"Phil, can I talk to you for a few minutes?" he questioned.

"Sure," Phil responded. "What's up?"

"I've been looking over the ambulance and it's in pretty bad shape," he complained.

"How's that?" Phil asked.

"Well, it needs washing and the inside needs cleaning out," he answered.

"That's strange. I thought we had been doing a good job of taking care of it," Phil replied.

"Well, obviously, you're not," Supervisor Carl sharply retorted.

"Maybe you can keep the damn thing lookin' better," Phil replied with a matching tone.

"Yeah, I think so. Or we'll get someone who can. You're through Phil. You're fired!" the Supervisor angrily said.

Always wanting to say the last word, he hotly replied, "You can't fire me. I just quit!" He turned on his heel, and walked to the living quarters to pack his clothes.

A thousand questions ran through Phil's mind as he packed his belongings and prepared to leave the work place. What was he gonna' do now? How was he going to be able to pay his car payment and his room and board? He consoled himself by thinking about joining the military.

These, and many more questions, ran through his mind and troubled him. He tossed the last of his clothes into a suitcase and headed to his car.

Several weeks passed during which he actively read Want Ads looking for work. Finally, after much searching, he ran into a former school buddy who worked at a manufacturing company. He told Phil they were looking for employees and he should go and apply. Phil immediately rushed over and submitted an application.

Two weeks later, the firm notified him he had been hired. He was instructed to report for work the following Monday. Breathing a sigh of relief, he was pleased most of his problems had been solved; his prayers had been answered.

The first week at work Phil was very dissatisfied with the job; he remaindered himself, he was receiving a salary. The largest he had ever earned. He was working the swing shift. He wasn't especially fond of the hours, nevertheless, it was a means to a livelihood, and to pay the bills.

A co-worker, named Harvey Moore, introduced himself to Phil. He said he liked to be called Harve. Both were young, single, and woman crazy. Having much in common, they soon became good friends who would stop after work, at a local bar, and have several beers, they jokingly referred to, "for the road" before leaving the bar, and always "another for the ditch."

Working together for a while, Phil and Harve soon got to know two female co-workers, who also worked in the production department. Although Phil and Harve didn't know it at first, the two females were sisters. Sharing the employee lounge, during breaks and lunch times, the four of them became friendly, telling jokes and laughing.

After knowing them for a couple of months, the sisters Andrea and Veronica, agreed after work to have a drink with them. Flattered by the two young men's attention, they needed little encouragement or persuasion to participate, in a seemingly harmless social activity, to have a good time.

Neither Phil nor Harve, both single, bored, and looking for female companionship, were aware of, or cared, about consequences resulting from entertaining married women. Their relationships seldom lasted for over a year.

The husband of one of the sisters found out about his wife's unfaithfulness. Hiring a private detective to investigate, he soon learned Harve was his wife's lover. He approached Harve and warned him to "stay away from my wife, or you will face serious consequences and big trouble."

Harve, in the prime of his youth, laughed it off and didn't take the threat seriously. He and Phil continued to meet, play with, and entertain the wives in a little, secluded bar called "Come on Inn".

One Saturday evening the four had met for a rendezvous, and were playing shuffle alley for amusement. At the end of the game one of them had gotten a rather low score of 312 points out of a possible 500. The number 312 score coincided with the employee number of 312, assigned to Phil at their place of employment. They all enjoyed a hearty laugh at the coincidence.

As a climax to the evening, the couples decided to go to a motel close to the younger sister's home, since both husbands were miles away, out of town. Each having their own car they drove to the motel, and rented a room. Veronica parked her car directly in front of the rented room. They continued partying, drinking beer from a twelve-pack they had brought with them.

In the early hours of Sunday morning a loud knocking on the motel door awakened them. A masculine voice was yelling, "Veronica! Are you in there?"

Panic filled the room. Veronica jumped from bed, putting her finger to her lips for silence, and whispered, "That's my husband."

The voice continued to yell, "On my way home I saw your car in the parking lot. I know you're in there!"

The noisy yelling brought the motel manager to the room the husband was standing in front of. The manager was heard to say, "Sir! Stop your yelling! You will wake up all our guests!"

"I don't give a damn about your guests! My wife is in this room with a lover!" "I'm trying to get her to come out!" He continued to yell.

Veronica moved to the doorway and spoke through the closed door. "John, go on home. I'll be there in a few minutes. We can discuss this there." She said, answering her husband's demanding voice."

"You damn well know we will!" he angrily said. Silence filled the air, until the sound of spinning tires and burning rubber broke the early morning stillness.

Phil and Andrea quickly got dressed. He drove her home, stopping a block from her house, to avoid any possible further confrontation, with another irate husband.

Monday morning Veronica showed up at work with a bruised and swollen face, and a black eye, camouflaged by mascara. It appeared she and her angry husband had interacted, with more than a discussion.

Going to his car that afternoon, after work, Harve found a note on the windshield that read "This is your second warning. Stay away from my wife, or I will kill you!"

Harve turned the note over to the police, and filed an Incident Report, but was told without a name or witness, the report would simply be filed, with no arrest.

For weeks after the incident, quickly forgetting the seriousness of the husband's angry encounter, Phil and Harve would unexpectedly come up behind one another and say, "Stay away from my wife, or I will kill you!" while loudly laughing.

Meetings with the sisters didn't actually stop, but they became much more cautious, about being openly seen together, and secretly met.

In the following months both Phil and Harve drank heavily. They would even sneak out of the building on work breaks and lunch hours to guzzle beer at one of the local gin mills. They became known by co-workers and friends as the "Drinking Duet."

While working with another co-worker Phil met a young man who, by his own admission, said he didn't drink, smoke, curse, and would walk away, when someone started to tell a dirty joke. From all outward appearances he did not display any obvious vices. He was obviously a Christian. He was teased by Phil and Harve, who tried to influence him, but, at the same time, the co-worker named Bill Stolz was beginning to influence his two fellow employees.

Bill would speak to them during breaks and lunch times about the hereafter, and their spiritual salvation. Harve would laugh and joke over Bill's concern, and out of his hearing, would refer to Bill as a "Holy Joe."

Phil didn't think it was right to joke and laugh about someone's convictions, and on several occasions attended church with Bill. Not wanting his going to church to become habit forming, he started begging off, when Bill invited him, making excuses as to why he couldn't attend.

CHAPTER 12

Persuasive Teaching

After his nineteenth birthday, Phil moved from his mother's home to a studio apartment close to his work. Now working full time on the day shift, he punched in at seven o'clock and worked until 3:30. This gave him a lot of free time. He idled the hours away with his buddy, Harve, drinking beer, shooting pool, and chasing women.

His high school days of participating in competitive drag racing, hot rodding, and "powerful souped-up" engines continued to capture his interest. He became acquainted with a young man name Earl Wetzel, who worked at a speed shop, specializing in racing equipment, and repair work on street legal racing cars. Phil had spent money "souping up" his Cadillac with dual carburetors, or "twin pots," as he liked to call them. He also had replaced the stock heads, with racing heads. Through this friend, Earl, he met his sister, Evelyn.

Evelyn looked familiar to Phil. Having met several times when she was visiting her brother at the garage, at the same time he was visiting Earl, he learned through their discussions she had been a student at the same high school Phil attended. He searched his memory as to why he couldn't remember her, while both were students, especially if she was half as attractive then, as she was now.

As days and weeks passed, Phil often visited Earl, seeking his advice and suggestions, on how he could "rev up" the Cadillac engine, for better performance, and more speed.

During those visits, Evelyn would come to the garage, from her parents' home located across the street from the garage, to visit her brother. Phil and Evelyn became better acquainted and he asked her for a date.

"Evelyn, I realize I hardly know you, but I would be honored if you would go out with me on a date," he invited.

"I would like that Phil, but I will have to ask my mother if I can," she replied.

"Ok, I would appreciate it if you would ask her, and let me know," Phil said.

"I will, Phil. I'll let you know the next time I see you," she assured him.

"I'll be looking forward to your answer. Hope it's good," he said smiling.

Phil was thinking, "I've never dated a girl who could not, or would not, make her own decision concerning dates. But he had never known a girl like Evelyn. He would soon learn Evelyn was not like other girls; she was a dedicated Christian.

When Evelyn asked her mother for permission to date Phil, she gave a flat, emphatic "No!" It appeared his reputation had proceeded him to the ears of Mrs. Wetzel, a staunch church goer. Through her son Earl, she had heard of his wild lifestyle, of partying, drinking, and associating with the wrong type of female companions.

When told of this Phil was sorry. He told her he didn't know what he could do to erase the past. Although hurt by the mother's decision and opinion, he respected the mother's stand for the safety of her daughter. Not easily dissuaded he knew he would ask her again.

Learning of the family's strong ties to church, he decided to approach her in another direction. The next time, he would ask Evelyn if he could take her to church.

The week before Easter Sunday he decided to ask her, if she would go to church with him on Easter Sunday. Monday of Easter week, after work, he dropped by the garage to visit Earl. While they were discussing different gear ratios for the best racing results, Evelyn casually came into the garage to let Earl know dinner was ready.

Phil was pleased to see her again. Admiring her looks, he was amazed to suddenly realize he had not underestimated her beauty.

Evelyn greeted him with a smile saying, "Hi, Phil. How have you been?"

"Good", he replied, and asked, "How about you?"

"I've been good too," she replied.

"You're looking lovely, as always," he said, complimenting her.

"Thank you, Phil," she said blushing, graciously accepting the compliment.

Earl interrupted their conversation by turning to Evelyn and saying, "Tell Mom I'll be right over for dinner as soon as I wash up."

"I'll tell her," replying to Earl, and then to Phil, "See ya' Phil," she said, and turned to leave.

"Just a minute, Evelyn. I want to ask you something. How about letting me take you to church on Easter Sunday?" he invited.

"That sounds like a wonderful idea. I'll ask Mom if I can go with you," she replied

"Good. Let me know what she says," he answered.

"I'll see you before then," she said, turning and running toward her home.

Phil was excited and pleased she hadn't said 'no,' and seemed anxious to go with him. He sincerely hoped her mother would not object to her going to church with him.

Phil told Harve about the new girl he had met, and that he was hoping to take her to church Easter Sunday. "She sounds like a "Holy Hannah" to me; you better watch out or you'll be getting' religion," Harve said laughing.

"You know, Harve, that just might not be a bad thing," Phil answered, disappointed Harve laughed at him, and his conviction of wanting to do the right thing, exercising his freedom of belief.

On Wednesday after work Phil went to the garage to visit with Earl and found out he was on a service call. So Phil chatted with one of the other mechanics on duty. Bored, he decided to leave when he noticed Evelyn come out of her house and start walking to her car not seeing him.

"Hey!" he called out across the short distance trying to get her attention

"Oh, hi Phil!" she called back, getting into her car and pulling up alongside.

"What did your Mom say?" he asked

"She said it would be ok," she answered.

"Terrific! What time does your church service start?" he asked.

"Eleven o'clock", she answered.

"Good. I'll be at your home about 10:30 on Sunday," he replied.

"I have to go to the grocery store, Phil. I'll see you before then. Bye Phil," she said before driving away.

He was pleased he was going to see her in just four days, even if it meant having to go to church. When Phil confided in Harve about his date on Easter Sunday he took quite a ribbing from Harve, and later from other co-workers, because Harve betrayed his confidence and told others about his upcoming date with a "Holy Hannah." It hurt Phil deeply to think his friend had betrayed his confidence, but he took it in stride, knowing they meant no harm, he took the brunt of the kidding with a smile.

For Phil, it seemed like Sunday would never get there. But suddenly it arrived. The shattering sound of the alarm broke the stillness of Easter Sunday. It seemed like the middle of night to him since he usually slept until early afternoon on Sunday. But today was not a usual Sunday for Phil. First it was Easter Sunday Morning, and second, he had a date with a very lovely lady.

He jumped from bed, and headed to the shower. He was nervous dressing for church, putting on clothes he rarely wore; a white shirt, gray tie, and dark blue suite. Combing his hair, he looked in the mirror and smiled approvingly at his reflection.

Arriving at the Wetzel home at 10:20, he pulled into the drive. Getting out of the car he straightened his tie, and smoothed imaginary wrinkles from his suit. Closing the car door, he anxiously walked to the front door and rang the bell, softly whistling while he waited.

The door opened and Evelyn greeted him, "Good morning, Phil. Come in. My, how nice you look," she said complimenting him.

"Thank you," he replied accepting the compliment.

"I would like for you to meet my parents," she told him. She led him through the foyer and into a spacious living room. An elderly gray-haired man sat on the sofa reading the Sunday paper.

"Dad, I would like for you to meet a friend of mine, Philip Kingsley," she said introducing him. "Phil, this is my father, Ed Wetzel".

"Nice to meet you, Sir," Phil said extending his hand.

"Good to meet you, Phil," her father returned the greeting.

"Come on, Phil, I'll introduce you to my Mother," Evelyn said, leading him into the kitchen.

The same formalities were performed as Evelyn introduced him to her mother.

"It's nice to meet you, Phil," the mother greeted him. "I was so happy you invited Ev to go to church with you this Sunday.

"It's my pleasure, Mrs. Wetzel," Phil said, returning her greeting.

"Well, Mother, we need to go. We'll see you in church," Evelyn commented. "Come on, Phil. let's go."

"My. It's almost time. By the way, Phil. We'd like you to have dinner with us if you don't have other plans," Mrs. Wetzel invited him.

"I would consider it an honor, Mrs. Wetzel," Phil replied, accepting the offer.

"Walking to the car Phil was careful to remember his manners to open the door for her, giving her plenty of time to get seated before closing the door.

Walking into the community church with Evelyn on his arm, he was aware of curious eyes following their every move. While being in church was not new to Phil, he somehow felt different in this extremely large sanctuary. Evelyn explained it was a community hall, being used as a church until the congregation could afford to have a church be built. It seemed strange to Phil for such a small group of people coming together, in such a large facility that would have seated five times the number of people present.

Phil enjoyed singing the hymns and joining in the worship service. He was pleased to be recognized as a visiting guest. He received a warm acceptance with many congregants extending a welcoming hand. It was so different from what Phil had been accustomed to. Even the message, or sermon, as it was called by the pastor was different. He was remembering how most preachers he had listened to were always talking about "hellfire and brimstone" and "eternal damnation", where this pastor was talking about the crucifixion, burial, and resurrection of Jesus Christ.

At the conclusion of the service the pastor did not beg for unsaved sinners to come forward and repent, instead, he opened the invitation altar call in an unemotional and rational manner by saying "Maybe there are those here this morning without Christ as Savior".

He was impressed as the small choir softly sang a hymn, while the pastor conducted the altar call, asking for heads to be bowed, and

Christians to be praying, for those, if any, without Christ, that they would turn to Him, and make Him their Lord today.

Phil felt uneasy, like he should go forward, but was too embarrassed to do so. The invitation ended; the Benediction prayer was offered, and church was dismissed.

The order of service had been completely different from what Phil had experienced, but he dismissed the thought by reasoning, this must be why there are so many churches.

The pastor made a special effort to meet him, warmly greet him, shake his hand, and invited him back to all of the church's services. It made Phil feel good and welcomed to the fellowship.

The rest of the afternoon passed quickly and pleasantly for Phil. He felt he really got to know Evelyn and her family over lunch, and secretly hoped, anything bad they may have heard about him had been overcome, by his friendly nature, gracious manner, and respectful attitude, while a guest in their home

To Prove a Point

Returning to work Monday, Phil was confronted with curious co-workers wondering about his Sunday date. He explained he had an enjoyable day and, consequently, he was not suffering from a hangover as many of them were.

In his ignorance of church gatherings, Harve gave Phil the worst time. He repeatedly reminded Phil "if he didn't watch out, he was gonna' get religion." Always scornful, he continued, "For me, I really can't see the good of going to church. They say, 'you can't do this, and you can't do that,' and they always have their hand out for your money."

He didn't stop there, he continued, "About the closest I ever got to church was when I was about twelve years old. I, and another kid, stole a gumball machine from in front of a store. We used a church lawn to break open the ball, and steal the money," he bragged, with a loud laugh.

Phil remained silent not wanting to reply to Harve's comments, and refused to be amused at his childish, long ago mischief. Harve was not finished with his criticism of church. Trying to convince Phil he was wasting his time going to church, he said, "As a matter of fact, I don't even believe in Heaven or Hell. I think there is enough hell right here on earth," he finished his criticism of church teachings.

Not wanting to argue, Phil simply said," Well, that's one of the nice things about a Democracy. Everyone is entitled to an opinion." He turned and walked away.

Several days passed before Phil saw Evelyn again. He could not forget how he had really been impressed, at the harmony which presented itself in the Wetzel home. And the peace of mind they seemed to enjoy, plus the attitude of humility outwardly displayed. He looked forward to again enjoying both Evelyn's and her parents' company.

One early evening, he stopped by the garage to see Earl. Evelyn happened to be there. Seeing her, Phil completely forgot what he wanted to talk to Earl about, and instead, spent time in conversation with her.

"Hi Phil. How are you?" she asked in a friendly voice.

"I'm good Ev," he replied, thinking he now knew her well enough, to call her by the nickname her mother used. "It's nice to see you again," he added.

"Thanks. Same here, Phil," she answered.

"Say, Ev, how about going out for a sandwich and a malt this evening?" he invited.

"That would be fun. The folks are going out to a restaurant for dinner. I didn't plan to go with them, and I hate to eat alone," she said, accepting his invitation. "Wait here a few minutes. I'll go tell Mom where we are going."

"OK. I'll be here," he promised.

She returned shortly, having placed a scarf over her head because Phil had put the top down. Driving into town they "cruised the gut' before pulling into a drive-in restaurant. A scantily clad waitress rolled up to the car, on roller skates, and asked to place their order. They each ordered cheeseburgers and chocolate malts. Waiting for the food Phil turned on the radio and selected a station with soft, romantic music. The food soon arrived. The waitress placed the burger and shakes on the tray, supported by hanging on to the car window. Enjoying the food Phil said, 'Well, this isn't exactly the Ritz, but it's a good substitute, with soft music, a moonlit night, and a scrumptious cheeseburger."

"It's fine. But you forgot to mention, good company," Evelyn said, laughing.

"Yeah. I did, didn't I?" Phil replied, joining her in laughter.

Phil noticed she had briefly paused before starting to eat the food. His family church upbringing reminded him she had offered a blessing in prayer before eating. He then knew, aside from her physical beauty, this was one of the characteristics he liked about her. The way she was not ashamed to express her convictions regardless of where she might be.

The crisp voice of a news commentator broke into the music, "We interrupt this program to bring you a special news bulletin, of a pending international crisis, concerning the controversial 38th Parallel.

"The second free election, scheduled for May 30, 1950, in the Republic of South Korea, is causing increased concern for United Nation leaders. The question is, will this democratic action further antagonize aggressive action on the part of Communist North Korea? Or, will it stimulate the people of the Northern side of the 38th Parallel, of this divided county, to demand equal opportunities?" "This is a developing story; this station will keep you advised of current events as they happen. This has been a Special News Bulletin. We now return to regular programming." Again, soft music flowed from the dual speakers.

Although silent about the news bulletin, his mind was deep in thought pondering the consequences of the so-called "cold-war." He had been following the accounts of the U.N. and Communist action concerning North and South Korea. He was very aware he was in direct line for Draft Status in the event of a national crisis.

"A penny for your thoughts," Evelyn said, breaking the silence.

"They're really not worth a penny," he replied, and continued, "I was just thinking about the seriousness of the world situation, and the part I might have to play in the event of a national crisis," he answered.

"It certainly doesn't look good," Evelyn agreed. "Do you think you would be called up, if there is a war?" she asked.

"There's no doubt about it. I'm classified 1-A. and I'm about to be drafted, anyway," he answered. He made a mental note to check with the local draft board to see where he stood in line to be actively drafted.

"We surely need to be praying this will work out for the best." Evelyn commented.

"Yes, we should. That's the least, and the most we can do," Phil agreed. He was amazed at the way Evelyn's life completely revolved around providential guidance, and Divine leadership.

Glancing at his watch, Phil was surprised to see it was past nine o'clock. "Wow! Time passes quickly when you're having fun!" he exclaimed. "I better get you home, Ev. Your parents will probably be home by now, and wondering where you are."

Phil was again thinking about just how fast time had gone by. He and Evelyn had spent more than two hours in idle chatter although it seemed only a few minutes.

Only a few words were exchanged on the way to Evelyn's home. Each appeared to be lost in their own thoughts. Arriving at the Wetzel home Phil pulled into the driveway and shut off the engine. Turning to Evelyn he said, "Well, Ev. I hate to say good night, after just saying hello. But I know you must get in. Thank you for the date. May I ask you to go to your church with me this Sunday?"

"You're welcome, Phil. Yes. I had an enjoyable time, and yes, I can go to church with you this Sunday," she replied accepting the invitation. They held hands as he walked her to her door.

"Until Sunday, then," Phil said.

"Yes. I will see you Sunday. Good night, Phil," she replied.

Phil's mind was in turmoil driving home to his apartment. Thinking out loud, he heard himself say, "Here I am, almost twenty years old and I haven't accomplished a thing in life. I don't have any money saved, and no prospect of saving any. And now, this threat of war hanging over my head."

I sure wish I had gone into the Army and started fulfilling my military obligation. Arriving at the apartment he emptied his mind of thoughts with a flippant exclamation, "Oh, well! No use crying over spilled milk!"

At work the next day, Korea was the topic of discussion, on the job, in the cafeteria, lunch room, and break room. There were those who were even betting as to whether the United States would get involved in South Korea's defense. Harve appeared quieter than usual. Phil asked, "What's wrong, Harve? You're so quiet today?"

"I'm just thinking, if the US does get involved in this conflict, my National Guard Infantry Battalion might be activated," he answered.

"I didn't know you were in the National Guard, Harve. How long have you been a member?" Phil asked.

"Two years. When I joined, the Draft Board changed my Classification from 1-A to "Ready Reserve, removing me from the draft list," he answered.

"That's great, Harve. You can't be drafted into the Army, because you are already a member of the military." Phil complimented him.

"Yeah, I guess so. It's been a good thing in one way. I've earned a few bucks on the side, and I've built up rank to Sergeant First Class, in case I'm activated. The weekly meetings, and the two weeks Summer Camp of Active Duty is a pain in the ass, though," he complained.

"Well, Harve, you can't have your cake, and eat it too!" Phil remarked by quoting a worn-out expression.

"You're a Class Act," Harve replied, closing his fist and lightly punching Phil's shoulder.

Phil didn't enter into the talk of war discussions. Because of this he was ostracized by associates and co-workers, who grew cold and indifferent toward him. Little did Phil realize the coldness, and indifference would turn to bitterness, hatred, and scorn a few weeks later.

After work, along with Harve, he had become accustomed to joining some of the "boys," at one of the local bars. Recently, he had been just stopping in for a beer or two, and then going straight home. The co-workers made a big deal of teasing him out of this. They attributed the reason to be, because he was dating a "Holy Hannah."

Phil was disturbed by the kidding, but took the ribbing with a grain of salt, grinned, and bore it. He was disappointed they choose him to be the butt of their jokers, but he knew they really meant no harm.

The teasing became more disturbing during the rest of the week. Harve, not satisfied to let it stay just between the guys, took it on himself to tell some of the female employees, including Veronica and Andrea who joined in the playful banter. One went so far as to caution Phil, "that he needed to be careful or he was gonna' get religion and marriage."

Phil wondered what was bad, or wrong, about either of the things she mentioned. But kept silent, because of the cynical way it had been mentioned. The manner in which the caution, or warning, if you could call it that, had been stated, caused both conditions to be distasteful.

On Friday, employees were complaining of a "Test Alert" sponsored by the Civil Defense Agency, scheduled for 3:45 PM, fifteen minutes after quitting time. Management explained the purpose of the "Alert" was, to use as many of the Civil Defense evacuation routes out of the city as possible, the goal being to evacuate the entire city within two hours. Many employers had been requested to participate in the "Alert."

The chief employee complaint was, the "Alert" was going to throw them off schedule and detain many, who drove long distances to and from work, from getting home to pick up their children from day care.

Phil was not concerned because he lived within a block of the plant where he worked. He was nervous and keyed, up due to the frustration expressed by co-workers about the "Alert" and all of the joking and kidding he had had to endure about his private life. Clocking out, he headed out of the plant to his apartment. He heard a voice behind say, "If you'll stop at the Stadium, I'll buy you a drink."

He stopped and turned to see Andrea catching up to him. Past times flooded his memory; he was in just the right mood. "Maybe a drink is just what I need," he said, accepting her invitation.

"That sounds great. I'll see you there in about thirty minutes," he said.

Reaching the apartment, he showered, shaved, and applied his favorite after shave. Walking to his car he remembered the "Alert" and became aware of sirens going off around him. He entered the line of cars leaving the city, hoping he would not be too late to join Andrea.

The slow-moving line of traffic eventually reached the turn off to the "Stadium Inn," so-called because it was direfully across the street from the "Kingston Baseball Stadium.

Walking in to the bar he saw Andrea seated in a corner booth with two drinks sitting in front of her. He could see she was on her second drink because of an empty glass on the table.

"Sorry I'm running late. Because of the "Alert" traffic was a mess," he apologized.

"Hi friend, be seated and drink up. Only ten hours to go," she said, greeting him.

"Only ten hours? You don't plan on drinking 'til closing time, do you?" Phil challenged her.

"Why not? My old man is out of town and the kids are with the grandparents. Let's drink up and be merry," she replied.

This was not the way Phil had planned it, but figured he didn't have an alternative since he had accepted her invitation. He did not really want to drink to the point of getting drunk, but on the other hand, neither did he want to alienate Andrea by not drinking with her. He decided to "nurse" his drink and let her do most of the talking and drinking.

"What's the matter Phil? You're lagging behind. Come on; drink up," she encouraged him.

Phil had barely touched his drink when she slid her empty glass across the table and said, "I'm drinkin' gin and tonic. You order; I'm payin'."

He summoned the cocktail waitress and placed the order. Returning shortly, she placed the drinks on the table in front of them.

"You'd better slow down; you're going to get tight before you know it," Phil cautioned.

"Good. I want to get tight," she answered.

"Ok. Have it your way," Phil said.

"I will," she cheerily said, getting up and stating, "Excuse me; I gotta go to the little girls' room."

Waiting for her return, Phil reminisced about the so-called "good times" in the past, he had enjoyed in Andrea's company. Never a dull moment, she was a lot of fun to be with, he remembered.

Returning after a few minutes, she slid into the seat next to him sitting very close. His emotions were stirred by the closeness of her warm body.

"Phil. What's this I hear about you dating a "Holy Hannah?" she jokingly asked.

"No big deal. I just been seeing a young lady, who is a Christian. That's all there is to it," Phil answered.

"To hear co-workers talk, one would think you was getting religion, and marriage too," Andreas said, repeating almost word for word what her sister, Veronica had said about him.

"Well. You can hear anything," Phil said, defending himself. To lift his spirits from a low ebb, he tossed off his drink, and signaled for the waitress to bring another.

While in the beginning he had intended to "nurse" his drinks, he now found as the evening progressed, he was tossing them down as fast as Andrea, who was still going strong.

As hours passed, Andrea became happier, louder, and more flirtatious. Now sitting so close to him he had difficulty lifting his arm to bring the drink to his lips. By midnight, neither he nor Andrea were feeling any pain. Andrea was practically sitting on his lap. He decided it was time for them to go.

He drained his drink from the glass, threw a tip on the table, and suggested they leave. Andrea didn't need much prompting. She quickly got up, and tossed her jacket around her shoulders. Walking unsteadily from the bar to the parking lot, they climbed into Phil's car.

As soon as they were in the car Andrea had her arms around his neck and was rubbing her thighs against him. Resisting as long as possible, he gave in to rising passion. He pulled her to him, seeking her lips. They exchanged lip and tongue kissing for a full five minutes before she pulled away.

"Oh Lord! Let's go someplace!' she demanded. Starting the engine Phil drove to a place popular among teen-agers called "Rocky Point Cliff." The cliff offered a panoramic view of the city lights, although the participants were not interested in sightseeing. Rocky Point Cliff had become known as a "lovers' rendezvous."

Phil guided the car into a seldom used entrance concealed by a clump of brush on to a rutted dirt road running for a short distance abruptly ending at a forest edge. He turned off the lights and shut off the engine. Again, Andrea's arms were around him, seeking his kisses. He responded by kissing her lightly at first, and then drew her to him, crushing her lips beneath his, running his tongue in and out of her mouth. Climbing into the back seat, they slipped out of their clothing. Breathing hard, their warm, naked bodies came together in the coolness of the night. Afterwards, they lay side by side, exhausted and sobered, by energy spent in the act of adultery.

It was 1:30 AM when Phil drove Andrea to her car. He felt an inward sense of shame and guilt for what had happened. Parking the car, and walking to his apartment, he was totally unaware of the early morning hour. Anxious for the comfort of his bed, and the escape from reality sleep offered, he undressed hurriedly and fell across the mattress. He was in bed only a few minutes until the ceiling started spinning, and swirled above him. The longer he lay in bed, the faster the ceiling swirled. Tossing, and turning, he soon realized sleep was not coming.

Getting up, he went to the kitchenette and set a big pot of coffee to boil. Returning to the combination living room and sleeping area of the apartment he switched on the television hoping to catch a late, late movie playing. The shrill whistle of a bomb and the reverberating, tumultuous sound of its blast filled the tiny apartment as it burst forth from the television speaker.

"Great! That's is all I need! A war picture," Phil complained, grumbling aloud. He quickly turned off the television.

Hearing a buzzing sound letting him know the coffee had perked, he went back to the kitchenette and turned off the coffee maker. He generously poured a cup of strong, black coffee and cautiously sipped it. Finishing two cups he decided to give sleep another try.

Climbing back into bed, he pulled a sheet over him. This time the ceiling had stopped swirling, but had been replaced by the annoyance of a dull, throbbing ache beginning behind his eyelids, and spreading to the crown of his head. Jumping out of bed, he went to the bathroom, opened the medicine cabinet, washed down three aspirin, went back to bed and finally fell asleep.

He was awakened around 3 AM with an urgency to relieve himself. Taking care of nature's call, he returned to bed. Unable to go back to sleep his mind went back to the events of the evening. He knew he should not have been in the company of another man's wife, and certainly, not to have possessed her as only a husband was allowed to possess her morally, legally, and scripturally.

Reflecting back, he knew beyond the shadow of a doubt, he should have stayed home and not have accepted the invitation from Andrea. He was experiencing mixed, emotional feelings. While physically satisfied with the outcome, at the same time, he felt ashamed. Ashamed for giving in to passion, doing that which he should not have done, and for failing to do, what he should have done; resist surrendering to the temptation of a heated passion. He concluded his thinking by reasoning that, if he had stayed home, he would not now be struggling in having this battle with his conscious

Lying on the bed, staring at the ceiling, he prayed to God for forgiveness, "Oh, God, forgive me for what I have done. I know it was wrong, and I ask for your forgiveness."

In the days ahead, please help me to live a better life. A life that will not be in conflict with the powers of my own conscious." Closing his eyes, he uttered an "Amen". Finally, he dozed off into a peaceful sleep.

CHAPTER 14

A New Acquaintance

Phil was awakened by the sun's rays, streaming through the window, shining in his eyes. He frantically jumped from bed thinking he would be late for work. Picking up the day and date watch laying on the night stand, he was relieved to see the time was 11:15 AM and the day was Saturday.

Sitting on the side of the bed, he held his head in his hands, pressing his fingers to the temples in an effort to relieve the throbbing pain from a hangover. He remained seated, holding his head, until the throbbing subsided to a dull roar, exceeded only by the beating of his pounding heart.

Walking to the bathroom, he ran a glass of cold water; opening the medicine cabinet, he took out two Alka-Seltzer. Dropping them into the glass, he gulped them down as fast as they dissolved.

He paused to look at his reflection in the mirror. Talking to the reflection he muttered, "Oh brother! If I don't look awful?" His eyes were red and puffy; his complexion pale and drawn. He wondered just how many times he had told himself, the day after the night before, "this was the last time!"

But as he stared at his reflection, this time was different. He made a solemn pledge to himself that this would be the last time he drank to the point of getting drunk. Feeling hunger pains, he decided to shower, get dressed, and go out for breakfast. Refreshed, he walked a short distance to a local restaurant. He ordered a stack of hotcakes, two eggs, and a side of bacon, with orange juice, and a cup of black coffee. Feeling more relaxed, he leaned back against the cool leather of the booth and lit a cigarette.

He was on his second cup of coffee before the waitress brought the food. The smell of food almost made him gag. Quickly recovering, by taking small bites, and washing it down with the strong, black coffee, he began to feel better. He ate the remaining scraps of bacon, drained coffee from the cup, and drank half a glass of ice water. Placing a tip on the table, he got up, paid the bill, and walked out of the restaurant.

Back on the sidewalk he wondered what he should do for the rest of the day. He could go to his mother's home, but he knew there would be a lot of company there, and he didn't feel like visiting. Since his father's passing, it had become the recent custom, for some of the family members, to visit with her, on both Saturday and Sunday. His sister Mary had told him, their mother had been dating a male friend, off and on, for several months, and that, he also visited on week-ends, along with the family Phil was pleased to learn his mother was not isolating, and was seeing somebody. He was anxious to see them, especially his mother and her new male friend. He decided he would go to his mother's home to visit.

After putting the top down on the convertible, Phil climbed behind the wheel. Entering the highway, he picked up speed and enjoyed the cool breeze whistling through his hair. Having decided on what to do, he was beginning to feel better. It felt good to be alive; he appreciated the invigorating wind, swishing around the windshield brushing his face.

Wanting to lift his spirits, he turned on the radio, and pressed the selector bar, hoping to find some pleasant music to match his cheerful mood. The selector bar stopped. He heard the clipped tones of a commentator's voice giving a 1:00 PM news update. Quickly tiring of hearing local news, he again pressed the selector bar and held it in place, until he heard the word 'Korea.' He reached for the control and turned up the volume; the announcer's voice rose above the noise of wind in his ears.

"Relations between the United States and Soviet Socialist Communist governments are marked by mutual hostility. American and North Korean troops continue to clash at border points…"

Having heard enough, Phil turned off the radio. Suddenly, the full impact of the world situation dawned on him. He remembered, he never checked with the Draft Board, to find out where his 1-A classification date stood, before being drafted into the Army. Scolding himself for his negligence, he said aloud, "I have to do this on Monday."

Activities of the night before still weighed on his mind, and the recent news about North Korea, backed up by their Soviet Union ally, added to the heavy burden. The condition of not knowing, "the unknown," was a cause of great concern to Phil.

Arriving at his mother's place he noticed several parked cars he recognized. One he had never seen before. He recalled the information about his mother's male friend, and assumed that car must belong to him. When Phil entered the home, and walked to the dining room, everyone was seated around the table eating dinner. All were happy to see him, and he was warmly greeted. His mother called his attention to an elderly gentleman seated next to her.

"Phil, this is Jud Matthews, Jud, this is my son. Phil," she introduced them.

Jud extended his hand in greeting, and said, "Phil. How nice to meet you. I've heard many good things about you."

"My pleasure," Phil replied, wondering just what 'good things' he had heard.

"Have you had dinner, Son?" his Mother asked.

"I had a late breakfast, Mom. I'm not hungry," he answered.

"There's plenty here, if you want to join us," she insisted.

Sitting down in an empty chair he said, "I'll take some coffee, but I'm not hungry," he repeated.

His mother got up, went to the kitchen, poured a cup of coffee, returned and set it before him;

"Thanks, Mom," he said, as he started to sip the coffee.

Phil's brother-in-law, Alan, was a Veteran of WW II. Now, well past the age of draft, he was well-known by family members as the "joker," because he was always joking, and kidding.

Alan quizzically looked at Phil, "Phil, are you gonna' get that dread disease called, "Gone-to-Korea?" he asked, and broke out in laughter.

Phil enjoyed the play on words, and joined in the laughter, since he had only been looking at the serious side of a possible international crisis.

"Yeah, I guess so, Alan. Do you think it will come to that?" he asked, valuing input from a combat veteran.

"I don't know, Phil. But I do know this, if the United States had taught South Korea to use its military strength, as well as its economy, and culture, we would not be facing this situation today. Because, if the South Korean military was as well trained and equipped, as the North Korean military, this threat would not exist. As a veteran of war, I really can't conceive of any other outcome than the United States' intervention," Alan said, concluding his assessment.

"I think you are right. It sure doesn't look good for the country's sake. Again, Alan, I think you are right, but I hope you are wrong" Phil replied, respecting Alan's opinion. And repeated, "I hope you're wrong."

"So do I, so do I," Alan agreed.

Phil spent the rest of the afternoon in idle conversation with members of the family. He enjoyed the warm, informal times of fellowship, and friendship. He was thinking he should do it more often. Around 8 PM he decided to go home. Assuring Jud, it was good to have met him, shaking hands and giving hugs, he finally said good-night and left.

Driving home he thought of how impressed he had been with Jud Matthews. How nice it would be if his mother and Jud got married.

Even in the short time he had known Jud, and seen them together, they seemed like a good match. It would be good if she had a partner in her life. She had now been a widow for several years. Hadn't God created Eve, as a "help mate" for Adam? Well, those things have a way of working out, he reasoned, and concluded his thinking.

Arriving home, he pulled in under the shelter of a carport. He noticed dark clouds had formed in the east and it felt like rain, so he put the top up on the convertible.

Inside the apartment he raised a window to help eliminate the stale stuffiness. Turning on the television, he flipped through channels until he found a popular Western program. The soothing action of seeing other peoples' troubles solved, and acted out on the screen, had a relaxing effect causing him to become drowsy. He managed to stay awake to the end of the program, and then decided to go to bed early.

Reflecting on the activities of the day, he was pleased, and had enjoyed them, and was satisfied. He set the alarm for 9 AM, and undressed for bed. His thinking turned to tomorrow, remembering his promise to take Evelyn to church. As soon as his head hit the pillow, he fell sound asleep

CHAPTER 15

A Spiritual Awakening – Transformation

Phil was awakened by the shrill sound of the alarm piercing the stillness of the early Sunday morning. Then remembering the day's schedule, he quickened his movements, while he showered and shaved. He was unaware, of what lay in store for him, before the close of *this* particular Sunday.

After dressing, he decided to go out to eat at a small local restaurant known for its excellent breakfasts. Reaching the car, he debated whether to leave the top up, or put it down. The warm, brilliance of the sun, even at this early hour, quickly made the decision for him. Lowering the top, he recalled how last night it looked so much like rain. He was disappointed for not having received, but at the same time, was glad it had turned to such a warm, beautiful day.

Arriving at the restaurant he was pleased to see they were not busy. He ordered eggs, bacon, hash browns, orange juice, and coffee. The waitress brought a Sunday paper for him to read, while waiting for his order. Thoroughly relaxed, he enjoyed a delicious, nutritious meal.

Looking at his watch, he noted the time to be 10:30 AM. His reasoning assured him, he had plenty of time without being late, to enjoy the drive, to pick up Evelyn, go to church, and arrive just prior to the opening of worship. Behind the wheel and feeling good, he relaxed and let the warm wind massage his face.

Arriving at Evelyn's home he got out of the car, walked to the door, rang the bell and patiently waited. The door opened; Evelyn greeted him, "Good morning," Phil.

"Good morning, Ev," he said, returning the greeting.

"Come on in. I'll be ready in a few minutes," she invited.

Quickly re-appearing she said, "Ok, I'm ready."

Phil noticed she was carrying a small tape recorder. "Why the tape recorder?" he asked.

"It belongs to the church. The pastor asked me to start recording his sermons, so he could copy them off, and take to members not able to always attend church services. He called it a 'Shut In Ministry.'"

"Sounds like a good idea," Phil replied.

The organ and piano were playing, with the congregation standing, singing the Doxology, when they entered the church. Blending their voices in unison with others, they joined in the hymn praising God. The hymn ended; the congregation remained standing, waiting for the invocational prayer.

This was the order of service. A hymn, announcements, several hymns an offering was taken, and blessed with an offertory prayer. The preliminary worship service ended, and prior to the pastor's sermon a special musical presentation was presented, with an inspirational song sung by a soloist.

Standing behind the pulpit, the pastor paused, waiting for the undivided attention of the congregation. He then began his comments.

NOTE: His sermon is presented here, unedited and uncensored, from a copy of the recording Evelyn had tape-recorded at request of Pastor Ross.

NOTE: It is important to include the Sermon HERE because, it supports the decision Phil would make at the end of the Worship Service.

The SERMON: "If you have your Bibles with you, and I hope you do, please turn with me to the third chapter of the Book of Genesis."

"We will be reading verses 1 through 10. (After which, he asked God to invoke His blessing on the reading of His Word).

"The sweetest fellowship ever experienced by man was enjoyed by Adam; a fellowship that people have longed for ever since. The Bible says Adam in a moment of sin turned from God and even tried to flee from God, as God came to have fellowship in the cool of the evening.

"A sin in one's life should create a situation whereby man feels a need to draw closer TO God. However, Adam tried to flee God. This trend has continued throughout the centuries. The Bible says, in the Gospel of John, chapter 3, verse 20, 'For everyone that does evil hates the light, neither comes to the light, lest their deeds be reproved (meaning disciplined)'. John 3:20

"A man cannot flee from God. Adam found this out and so have others through the ages. The sinner, the backslider, the Christian can stay away from church, or fail to read the Bible, but he cannot flee God. Adam found this out approximately 3,000 years before then Apostle Paul, that God's Word says, in the book of Romans, chapter 2, verse 1, 'Thou, O man, are without excuse'.

"Every person without Christ will one day stand before God, and seek to justify himself. This is not true of the Christian. This will be true of the unsaved person, as they stand before God, and God brings up, and judges the secret life, the hidden things that you possibly have forgotten.

"So, then the question comes afresh to the unsaved person today, where are you in relationship to God and Christ? Are you ready, if that time comes today, and it very well might!!

"We know how we stand financially; this is not important. We know our social position. We know how we stand physically; these are NOT important!

ILLUSTRATION: "During WWII a fleet of convoy ships, after a mission, were traveling off the Alaskan coast. One of the ships, in the fog that engulfed them, strayed from the fleet, Unaware it was off course, crashed head on into a giant iceberg, bringing instant death to the sailors. Why? Because it didn't know its position.

ILLUSTRATION: "It is appreciated if you are on vacation, and someone tells you, that you are on the wrong road. Because you know that, every mile you travel in the wrong direction is costing you time, joy, and happiness.

"So it should be, when you are an unforgiven sinner, and someone tells you the Plan of Salvation Formula. It is revealed in the Apostle Paul's writing that there are only two roads you travel here on planet Earth; the NARROW, straight road, and, the broad, WIDE road."

ILLUSTRATION: "There was a certain young man, a sinner, whose Christian friends had been trying to persuade him to go to church with them. He had promised he would attend a revival meeting at a nearby church that very evening. He had consented and promised with NO INTENTION OF ATTENDING. That same evening he climbed on his motorcycle and headed down the road in the opposite direction from the church. While racing down the freeway he failed to see a slow-moving semi-truck and trailer. He ran into the truck at a high rate of speed, and was killed instantly.

"He had been offered opportunity to go to church, and get to know Jesus as his personal Savior, but he had tossed the opportunity aside, to pursue another interest."

"The Bible says, in the Gospel of John, chapter 3, verse 36, '*He that believes on the Son has everlasting life; and he that does not believe the Son shall not see life, but the wrath of God will condemn him.*'

"God asks the question; '*Where are you?*'

"Which side are you on today? Unless you are on the Lord's side and have accepted Him as your Savior, been baptized, and are faithful to God, you are on the WRONG Side. Without God's plan, you are an unforgiven sinner. Salvation means a literal about face. If you are following the enemy Satan, it means you will do an about face "and follow God."

ILLUSTRATION: "A child doing wrong in a parent's eyes usually will go to the parent and ask for forgiveness. Generally the parent will forgive the child; so it is with God. The sinners of the world today need to turn to God and say, 'Father, I am sorry. I am a sinner. I repent of my sin and ask you to forgive me. Dear Jesus, come into my heart, and become my Personal Savior. I make you the Lord of my life.'

"Very few people think they are sinners. That is the trouble with the world today; people are not thinking. Jesus Christ is a scarlet thread, which runs through this old book, (the pastor held up the Bible), from Genesis to Revelation. Take Him out, and you have nothing more than a book of ethics.

"After you accept Christ as your Personal Savior, you can through faith, resist the power of the enemy Satan. Not because of yourself, but because of what God has done for you. Then, and only then, can you have peace of mind, peace described in the Bible, in the Book of Philippians, chapter 4, verse 7 that says, '*The peace that passes all understanding*'.

"Those with sin-filled lives need to look to the cross, on which Jesus died, and see him there afresh this morning, as he hangs with outstretched arms, and begs you to cast your burdens on Him," the Pastor said, concluding the sermon, and inviting the congregation to stand.

The choir begin to sing, "Just as I Am", an altar call hymn of invitation.

Phil was under heavy conviction that the pastor had been preaching, only to him, throughout the sermon. His mind race back over his belief that he was a Christian, because of his upbringing, He now was struggling with the fact that he had little or no understanding or concept of God, or Christ from a personal perspective, consistent with what the pastor had been preaching about. And he realized, he did not have the "peace" of which the pastor had just spoken. Suddenly he realized, he was not a Christian at all.

The choir continued to prayerfully sing verses of the old familiar hymn. Phil felt a compelling need for conversion and the acceptance of "Jesus as his personal Savior. Finding his mind saying, "this is for you" he found himself mysteriously moving from the pew, to the center aisle leading to the altar, to accept the inviting hand of the pastor, as an indication he wanted to accept Christ into his heart as his personal Savior.

The invitation closed. The pastor explained to the congregants the reason Phil had come forward was for repentance, and to invite Christ to forgive him, and become his personal Savior.

Pastor Ross announced, "After the benediction, Phil will be standing with me at the exit. Please come by and extend a hand of fellowship for this very important decision."

In congratulating him, the congregants were very happy for Phil. But not as happy as Phil was for himself. In his own thinking, it was the happiest day of his life.

Phil was unaware, the giant step he had just taken, affecting an about face in his young life, would subject him to criticism, ridicule, scorn, and strong temptations put in front of him by his worldly associates, co-workers, and so-called friends. But due to his strong convictions, had he known, he would not have changed the decision he made. He now had a new friend named Jesus, and new-found faith in God.

CHAPTER 16

Tried and Tested

Monday was an ordinary day for Phil, as he went about performing his duties on the job.

Although life was not outwardly different, he was very aware of the things he had become accustomed to doing out of force of habit, which he now knew were wrong. In his mind he told himself he must think about, and prepare for how he was going to talk, so to no longer curse, or swear, especially not to take God's name in vain.

After work he decided to stop by the local Draft Board to check on his draft status date.

Since he got out at 3:30 PM, he would have time to get there before closing. He skipped going to the bar with the co-workers. They made a few snide remarks concerning his absence but he didn't bother to explain. At his early stage of Christianity, he did not hold any reservations about social drinking.

From the Draft Board he learned he was on the list of draftees to be inducted into the Army within the next thirty days. Although he halfway expected this news, he was discouraged, but at the same time, felt a sense of relief to know he would no longer have the draft status hanging over his head.

He was discouraged because he undoubtedly knew he would be involved in the Korean situation, if it resulted in an international crisis. He was relieved because he finally would be getting my military obligation over with.

The next day without telling anyone, he began getting his personal affairs in order. He had heard you could volunteer ahead of your induction date and the Draft Board had confirmed it. He was trying to make up his mind whether to volunteer so his name would be placed on the next group of draftees going for basic training in two weeks, or to wait until he was notified to appear for a physical

After receiving several responsible peoples' opinions, he decided he would volunteer. Calling the Draft Board to volunteer, he learned the next inductee call up date was in just two weeks. This meant he would have two weeks to notify his employer to get a Military Leave of Absence for active military duty, and call, or see all his friends, and tell them about going in the Army, and say good bye.

Having dropped out of high school, he was no longer a participating member of the "Dare Devil Club," and had resigned as president. He still wanted to let some of his former buddies know he was being drafted. He also wanted to let his friends Pat, and Eileen know, and especially say good bye to his former best friend Dave, and let him know he was being drafted. Thinking out loud, he heard himself say, "I'll have a very busy two weeks".

He didn't tell his co-workers he was getting a military leave of absence. But somehow it leaked out and became common knowledge. At about the same time his co-workers also found out he had become a Christian. He became the brunt of their jokes, ribbing, ridicule, and scorn.

One of the old-timers with whom Phil worked stopped him one day and said, "I hear you got religion, Son."

"You might say that. I accepted Christ as my Savior," Phil politely answered.

"Well, be that as it may, you'll never get anything unless you work for it. Look at me. I used to go to church in my younger days, and what have I got to show for it? Nothing!" he scornfully replied, answering his own question.

Not wanting to argue Phil answered, "You might start by counting your blessings."

"Whatya' mean? Blessings? Blessings?" the old-timer asked in a challenging way,

"Sir, you have your health, family, and a good job," Phil answered.

"Bah! Humbug!" the old-timer huffed and puffed, and in anger stomped off.

Others approached Phil differently. One young co-worker with whom he had become acquainted, and had gotten to like, came to him and said, "Well, Phil, ya' may have gotten' salvation, and the Lord may have your soul, but the Army will soon have your ass. Then, I'll give you about four weeks, to get off this religious kick."

"We'll see. We'll see," Phil replied in a confident voice.

Phil's friend, Harve, gave him the worst time. Laughing loudly, he approached Phil saying, "I hear you're on a religious kick, now. What are ya' gonna' give up?"

"What do you mean?" Phil asked.

"I meant things that are considered vices. Are ya' gonna' give up smokin'? How about cussin'? Are you gonna' quit cussin'?" Harve asked.

"Yes," Phil answered.

"How about booze; are ya' gonna' give up drinkin'?"

"Yes," Phil replied.

"Hey! How about women? Are ya' gonna' give up sex, too?" he continued to ask.

"Yes, I am; that too," Phil again said.

Harve was absolutely shocked by Phil's' answers, and remarked, "Man, you're gonna' give up cussin'; give up smokin' give up booze, and drinkin'; and give up women and sex!"

"Man! When are they gonna' bury you? You're dead, and don't know it!" Harve exclaimed.

"I'm very much alive. And, I'll be much better off to give up all of those, in your words, 'vices,' even if I wasn't a Christian," Phil pleasantly replied.

"It won't last! It won't last! This religious kick, I mean. I hear you're going in the Army pretty soon and "I'll just bet you'll be back to your old, sinnin' self, before ya' know it." Harve predicted.

"No. I don't think so," Phil answered.

"You just mark my word," Harve laughingly said.

"I'm not going to worry 'bout it. The Bible assures us that God watches after his own. I'm sure He will be lookin' out for me," Phil confidently answered

So the conversations ran, on religion as the chief topic of discussion, with Phil and his co-workers for the next two hectic weeks.

Phil and Harve usually got to the time clock to punch out at about the same time. After punching out and heading out of the plant, it had become a standard heckling joke for Harve to call our after him, "Phil. Don't drink too many milkshakes!'

The employees who had been made aware of Phil's transformation found humor in the joke and laughed heartily

While the last two weeks on the job had been trying and stressful, they just seemed to fly by for Phil. Before he realized it, Friday of the second week arrived. Standing in line, next to the time clock, to receive his final check from the Payroll Office, many of his fellow workers, in spite of all the kidding they had given him, now came to shake his hand and were sincere when they wished him well, and good luck in the military. It made him feel good to know they respected him enough to wish him well.

Having given a thirty-day notice, this was the last day he would be in his apartment. He had a lot to accomplish. He had made previous arrangements with his mother to store his household items in her garage to keep for him. She was not surprised when he showed up with his belongings. He had only a television set, bed, mattress, and bedframe, in the way of furniture. The rest was clothing, and other items of sentimental value.

Jud Matthews was there when he arrived. Phil noticed he had become a pretty steady visitor. Lately every time Phil visited his mother Jud had been there. He was pleased to know Jud was showing so much interest in his mother.

He spent the remainder of his civilian time saying good bye to friends and relatives. He called Eileen and learned she was getting married in a month. She was happy to learn Phil had become a Christin, and told him she also had become a Christian, and that her fiancé was in seminary, and on graduation was planning to work in the mission field.

Although connected only by phone they were happy to talk and catch up on what had been happening. Eileen wished Phil the best of luck and God's blessings before they said their good-byes.

Time had passed since Phil had been in touch with a lot of his acquaintances and friends. He found it time consuming in trying to locate them, because some had moved, were married, or were no longer listed in the phone directory, and some had even moved out of the state or country.

He especially wanted to connect with Dave, to renew their friendship, and to let him know he was leaving to join the military. After making the connection, Dave told Phil, he and Pat had gotten married, and were expecting their first child. Dave told Phil it was great to remember all the good times they had had together and urged him to stay in touch.

On Thursday of the second week he received military orders to report Saturday to the local Draft Board where he would join other draftees, for processing and then fly to a training center to receive basic training.

By Friday of that same week, he had contacted all of the acquaintances and had rekindled all the friendships he wanted to. He decided to call Evelyn to see if she would like to go to a movie with him. He had been seeing her at church, but had not told her he was going into the military.

Evelyn's mother answered when he called. He identified himself and asked to speak to Evelyn.

"Hello, Phil, how nice of you to call. I was thinking about you because I hadn't heard from you," she continued her greeting.

"Hi, Ev. Yeah, I've been pretty busy. The reason I called was, to ask if you would like to take in a movie this evening" he asked.

"I'd love to go. Wait a minute. I'll ask my Mom if it's ok," she replied.

He could hear her voice in the background talking to her Mother, but could not make out their conversation. In a few minutes he heard Evelyn returning.

"Mother said I can go, Phil. What time?" she asked.

"We'll be going to a drive-in movie. I'll be there about 7:30. The movie starts at 8 PM," he answered.

"Ok, Phil. I'll be ready," she assured him.

Phil picked Evelyn up at 7:30. On way to the drive-in theater Evelyn asked, "What have you been doing this week?"

"Not much. Just the usual things, but I have something to tell you," Phil answered.

"I'm leaving for the military tomorrow," he replied.

Evelyn was surprised at the news. "The military! You're kidding me!" she exclaimed

"No. No, I'm not. It's for real," he said, pulling a copy of his military orders from his pocket, he handed it to her.

"I can't believe it, Phil. It was just the other day we were talking about your having to go into the service."

"Yeah, I remember. But we never know what tomorrow holds in store for us," he answered.

"You're right, Phil. That's why it is so important to be ready," she agreed.

"If you had said that a month ago, Evelyn I would have inwardly laughed, but now I whole-heartedly agree with you. A good motto would be, 'Expect the best, but prepare for the worst.'

Having arrived at the drive-in they now sat in the car continuing to talk. Soon the setting of the sun turned the day to dusk and it was time for the movie to start. Holding hands, they relaxed in silence to enjoy the entertainment of the evening.

After the movie Phil and Evelyn stropped at a local restaurant for a light refreshment. Talking on the way home Evelyn said. "Phil. I'm sorry you will be leaving, but I know you have a military obligation. I wish you the best of luck, but more than that, I pray God's blessings will be with you. Please promise you will stay in touch. Will you?" she said, ending her comment with a question.

"I will, Evelyn. I'll be home on furlough after my basic training. I'll also see you then," he promised.

Sitting in the driveway, after arriving at Evelyn's home, she consented for Phil to give her a good night kiss.

Going over final departure plans, Phil suddenly realized, he had not made arrangements about leaving his car, which was now paid for, with a responsible party. He decided to let his younger brother Mark use, and be responsible for the vehicle in his absence. He smiled, thinking this action would resolve and erase any disagreements, or misunderstandings they ever had, and show he held no ill-feelings or resentment.

The next day, many of Phil's relatives were on hand to see him off, and to wish him well, with God's blessings. His mother and Jud, along with his oldest brother, James, and family, drove him to the airport.

Phil saw all the mothers, fathers, brothers, sisters, wives, and sometimes sweethearts, with moist eyes placing farewell kisses on their loved one, just before they boarded the military aircraft.

Phil felt a tightness in his chest as he turned to kiss his mother good-bye, and waved to other members of the family. He hated partings, especially this type of parting, where tears were shed. He was almost glad, when he heard the roar of the engines come to life, and the final announcement to fasten seatbelts for takeoff.

Through the window, he waved to the family, as the plane begin to taxi down the runway; soon they were airborne. Having experienced a safe take-off and becoming airborne the Captain's voice came over the speakers announcing seatbelts can now be released; smoking is permitted.

The aircraft was provided by the Air Force for the purpose of transporting troops and did not have the conveniences provide by commercial airlines. The interior consisted only of cold, gray unpadded seats.

Flying was a new experience for Phil, and he felt a sense of tenseness when the plane began to encounter turbulence. This combined with the smoke-filled air from almost all of the seventeen other young draftees nervously puffing on cigarettes. His tenseness began to ease, when another one of the group said "Hello," and extended his hand in greeting, and said, "I'm Frank."

"Hello. I'm Phil. It's good to meet you," he replied. Phil and Frank started talking in idle conversation.

Others on the plane kept to themselves, making a pretext of reading from the outdated magazines scattered around their seats.

Another draftee pulled a pack of playing cards from his pocket and looking around the plane asked, "Anyone for poker?"

Several responded by nodding their heads and moving over closer to the would-be dealer who identified himself as, "I'm Harry."

Phil finished looking at the magazine, tossed it aside and reached for a cigarette. He then remembered he had quit smoking. The draftee next to him noticed he was without cigarettes and offered him one. "Would you care for a smoke?" he asked.

"Oh. No. Thanks. I just recently quit smoking, and haven't gotten out of the habit of reaching for one," he explained.

"My name is Clark; what's yours?" the young man who had offered him a cigarette greeted him.

"I'm Phil, Phillip Kingsley," he answered, extending his hand in greeting.

"Why did you stop smoking?" Clark asked.

"Well, it's expensive for one thing, and it really doesn't do anybody any good for another," he replied.

He really wanted to explain the "real" reason he had given up smoking was due to his religious conviction. Instead, he explained, it was because he believed smoking to be wrong, and harmful to the body.

In fact, he was hesitant, to tell Clark the real reason for quitting was because of his religious belief, because he knew others were listening. Knowing he would be training with them, for the next thirteen weeks, he believed they would immediately brand him a "religious fanatic". He was not ashamed of his religious conviction, but felt such a branding would weaken his spiritual influence with his fellow trainees.

"Yeah. I guess you're right, Phil. I wish I could quit, but I can't," he replied.

"Sure you can, if you really want to," Phil assured him.

"I suppose so. But I never really had the desire to quit. More power to you, though. I admire your stand," he congratulated Phil. In the following days Phil and Clark became good friends.

Having nothing to do to occupy his mind, Phil rested his head against the seat, closed his eyes and dozed. He was awakened when the pilot's voice came over the intercom, announcing, "Fasten your seat belts; we are on the final approach for landing."

CHAPTER 17

Little Boys vs. Real Men

The draftees were met at the airport by a burley sergeant named Wilson, who lined them up, and started barking commands to them. Leading the way to the parking lot, he stopped the draftees, and in a strong, husky voice growled, "Line up in two rows, shoulder to shoulder, an arm's length apart."

Wanting to show his superiority he yelled, "You're in the Army now! God may have your soul, but the Army has your ass! So listen up! Pointing to a waiting truck he said, "We're gonna' load up in that US Army, 6X6, 2 ½ ton truck, and take you to your new home.

But first, we're gonna' have roll call. When your last, and first name is called, you answer, "Here, Sir!"

The Sergeant alphabetically called out the last, and first names of all eighteen draftees.

Satisfied all were present he said, "You are all little boys now. But the United States Army is gonna' make REAL men outa' you!

When I say 'Fall out!' You are to break from ranks, and load up in that truck, and we'll be on the way to your new home."

Finishing the instruction, at the top of his voice, he yelled "Fall out!"

Eighteen draftees, who were soon to be renamed 'Recruits' broke from rank, and scrambled to find a seat in the back of the truck.

Once they were seated, the Sergeant said, "Relax; I'll be back, I need a cup of java." Both he and the driver, disappeared inside the Airport Terminal.

In the boiling hot sun, under the shade of a trap covering the bed of the truck, the draftees impatiently waited. Three-quarters of an hour passed before the Sergeant and driver returned. The draftees had been introduced to a familiar comment in the Army; the comment of "Hurry up, and Wait!"

Arriving at the processing center they were given a physical examination, filled out paper work, vaccinated for malaria, and typhoid, and were then taken to the barber shop for a crew haircut. Then to the Quartermaster detail, where they were measured for size, fitted with uniforms, and boots, and issued a footlocker.

To Phil it seemed like a week had already passed by the time they were taken to the barracks, and told to "square away your gear." They were informed, "Mess Call for Chow will be at 1630 Hours."

Phil was not impressed with the barracks, where they would be living for the next thirteen weeks. But in his mind, he reasoned, "I'm so tired. Anyplace would be welcome, if I could just lie down and sleep." Little did he know, he along with the others, would be sleep deprived for the next thirteen-week duration of basic training.

After they had eaten chow they were instructed to "Return to quarters, where you will receive further instruction, on what you will face during basic training."

Back in barracks or "quarters" as the barracks were now referred to, the "Drill Sergeant" was introduced by Sgt. Wilson. "Listen up! This is Sgt. Baker," he said pointing to the sergeant. "The Drill Sergeant you will be responsible to for basic training. Just know, Sgt. Baker is a Bad Ass Drill Sergeant and will make real men out of you. Do what he says. Follow his directions and you'll get along just fine. Cross him, and you will wish you had never been born!! Did I get that right, Sgt. Baker?" he asked the Drill Sergeant.

"Yes. Yes, you did, Sgt. Wilson. I'm sure all of these brand new, never been used recruits and I, will get along great," he said, reinforcing Sgt. Wilson's cynical comments.

He thanked Sgt. Wilson, who quickly left the barracks. He gave the command of "At ease." And begin to give instruction, on what to expect during basic training. "An orderly will come by to instruct you on how to make a military bed, instruct you on how to square away your gear, and how to lay out your foot locker.

After you get your military bed made, and gear squared away, you will be dismissed for the rest of the evening. Reveille will be at 0500 Hours, (civilian time 5 AM), Mess Call in the Chow Hall at 0600 Hours, Barrack Inspection at 0700 Hours and then your day begins.

I'm sure we will all get along famously," he finished the instruction, introduced the orderly who had just entered the barracks. "Recruits, this is Corporal Johnson. He will continue with the instruction. Good night. Sleep fast, and well. I will see you at Reveille," he said, with a challenging grin, turned on his heel, and left the quarters.

Although he appeared to have a bulldog resemblance while standing before the recruits, Sgt. Baker's demeanor, and monotone voice seemed to be mild mannered. The recruits were in for a surprise, and would endure an exhausting, grueling, thirteen weeks of basic training, preparing them to be Infantrymen.

Following reveille and chow, Sgt. Baker conducted a quarters inspection stating, "You're first inspection will be a model that will be followed each and every day. Each inspection will identify you as to how well you follow orders. After making corrections, from today's inspection, your next assignment will be on the Parade Ground where you will learn the basics of facing movements and marching. You will then learn the fundamentals of hygiene and health from classroom instruction. At 1200 Hours, we will go to the Mess Hall and chow down."

Phil's mind wandered while the Drill Sgt. Baker's voice droned on, and on. Since military jargon, and terminology, (referred to by military personnel as nomenclature), was unfamiliar to the majority of recruits, it sounded like just so much gobbley-gook to them, but they were soon to learn.

The following weeks were so busy, Phil was hardly aware of the time of day, or for that matter, what day of the week it was. He was so stiff-jointed from the strenuous routine of the first week he could barely move.

They had been introduced to the so-called "Army Daily Dozen" which was twelve exercises done in repetition, day after day, consisting of everything from jumping-jacks to deep knee bends. The exercises (referred to by military personnel as calisthenics), ended with a "Cross-Country" run for approximately one-mile, over unimproved ground.

At the end of the second week Phil knew how to take apart an M-1 Rifle, and put it back together blindfolded. He had learned marching movements, and could do a left, right, and about face. He now knew how to do a "to the rear, March" and also execute a right or left column, or flank movement to the right, or left, and execute a left or right oblique movement. He felt good to know he could learn so much, in such a short time.

For the first three weeks, Sunday was the only day the recruits had free. They used this time to "shape up" their barracks, footlocker, gear, and uniform.

On Saturday, before the fourth Sunday, Phil planned to attend a Chapel Worship service held at 1100 hours, (he had learned to decipher, and start using Military Time). He intended to invite a fellow recruit he had befriended named Clark. Clark was shining his boots when Phil approached him and asked, "How's it going?"

"It's a rough grind, Phil. I never had so much discipline in all my life," he answered.

"Do you have plans for Sunday?" Phil asked.

"Probably sleep. I'm beat. Why do you ask?"" he answered, and questioned.

"Would you like to go to Chapel service with me?' Phil asked.

"What time is it?" Clark asked.

Phil answered, "1100 Hours," (starting to use military time), "you would still have time to get some rest and a good night of sleep, if you turn in early."

"Yeah, I would. Sure, I'll go with you, but you'll probably have to wake me up."

"I will be pleased to. See ya' in the morning. Good night; sleep well," Phil assured him, returned to his bunk and prepared for bed.

They enjoyed Chapel service and were glad they had attended. Following the service, they went to civilian café located on the base for breakfast and savored civilian food resembling "home cooking."

Back in quarters Phil suggested they write home, letting the folks know how they were getting along, which they both agreed to do. At the close of the fourth Sunday, with nine more weeks of basic training to go, both were pleased, having enjoyed a day unlike any they had known for a month.

Standing reveille, the following morning, in the grayness of dawn, dark clouds were forming, threatening rain, or as the military called rain, "inclement weather".

The recruits had been ordered by Drill Sgt. Baker to, "Assimilate your poncho under your web belt, on your back, in case of inclement weather." The poncho took the place of a raincoat, and was a square, waterproof material, with a hole in the center, to put the head through, designed to drape down over the fatigue uniform, which could be folded, up and placed under the web belt. Each recruit had been issued one, along with their uniform and equipment.

Arriving at the Parade Grounds the troops would drill for fifty minutes, and then would take a ten-minute break. This was one of the things Phil liked about the Army. Every fifty minutes there was a ten-minute break for those who smoked. The Drill Sgt. would command, "Fall out! Smoking lamps lit." While Phil no longer smoked, he really needed, and looked forward to the break time.

That particular day, during break time, drops of rain begin to fall, spattering the ground. Drill Sgt. Baker ordered the troops to break out their ponchos. Everyone followed his order except one recruit who had not gotten the "word" to "assimilate" his poncho. Phil found out later that the Army identified those who didn't get a message as the "ten percent who never get the word."

A full Colonel visiting dignitary checking the quality of instruction being given, rolled up in a jeep driven by a driver. The Colonel saw the young recruit sitting, and shivering in the now heavy downpour. Walking up to the recruit, the recruit jumped to his feet, stood at attention, and saluted, while the rain soaked his fatigue uniform.

Returning the salute, the Colonel asked, "Don't you have a poncho, Soldier?"

"No." came the recruit's reply.

"No WHAT Soldier?" the Colonel asked, expecting the recruit to say 'No Sir!'

"No poncho," the soldier replied, to the amazement of all who heard.

The Colonel pulled himself up to his full height, and said, "Carry on, Soldier! Carry on!"

"Yes Sir!" the recruit replied, giving the Colonel a snappy salute.

The Colonel's eyeballs bulged when he with a snap of the wrist, returned the salute and stormed off to his jeep and driver.

While there was much hard work and discipline, there occasionally was a humorous occurrence. Like the first time one recruit fell out for retreat.

Since this retreat was being held on this particular day honoring the Commanding General the uniform ordered was for Class "A," meaning cotton khakis.

Up to this time, many of the recruits had never tried on their Class "A" uniform, including a meticulous little Frenchman named Delatorre. Retreat for the Honoring Formation was being held after the work day, it meant the work uniform of fatigues, had to be changed to khakis in approximately fifteen minutes. All the recruit's in Phil's company were scurrying to and fro in an attempt to change uniforms. Recruit Delatorre who always looked his best, even in fatigues with starched creases on the back of his fatigue jacket, and highly polished boots, was completely dressed with exception of his trouser. Five minutes before falling out for retest Delatorre carefully removed his khaki trouser from the hanger and shoved his fete through the heavily starched legs.

A roar of laughter erupted when one of his comrades noticed the trouser legs stopped at the top of Delatorre's boots. Since it was Army regulation that trouser legs were to be bloused nine inches from the ground over the top of the boots, it would be impossible to blouse Delatorre's to regulation. Laughter spread. Many of Delatorre's fellow recruits laughed good-naturedly when they looked at his predicament.

Just then a whistle blew for them to "Fall out for retreat!" Delatorre pondered on what to do. He knew if discovered, he would be disciplined and reprimanded. But he also knew if he was absent from Retreat Formation, he would suffer a greater punishment. He decided to chance it.

The amusement of his comrades was difficult to control when he took his place in formation. In the distance music begin to play and the recruit platoon was called to attention, along with the Infantry Battalion and ordered to "Present Arms!"

Delatorre breathed a sigh of relief, as the Battalion Stood at attention, saluting the General, who stood in a jeep, with a white interior, returning the salute, while he was slowly driven, inspecting the troops.

Delatorre's relief was even greater when he heard the Battalion Commander "Order Arms!" Company Commanders, Dismiss your companies!"

He hastily fled the formation thankful he had not been "found out."

As weeks progressed, the work for the recruits became more demanding, and the duties less desirable. Each had their share of KP duty, latrine duty, scrubbing of floors, stoking of boilers, and of 'policing the grounds' (picking up paper and trash from the immediate barrack area), and Parade Grounds, in addition to their regular duties. Inspection in ranks, and in quarters, became more, and more "chicken shit" as the troops liked to call it.

One morning during Inspection in Ranks Drill Sgt. Baker was in a really bad mood because the day before, during the showing of a training film, someone had stolen his special fatigue cap. Since then, he had been wearing an old battered, and dilapidated cap, which looked as if it had survived the First World War I. The recruits could tell by the look in his eye, that he was going to be especially tough on them.

Calling the platoon to "Atten-hut!!" He ordered, "Open ranks!"

Instead of giving the 2nd, 3rd, and 4th, ranks "Parade Rest", he kept the entire platoon standing at attention while he took a slower than usual time inspecting the troops, starting with the 1st. rank.

He stopped in front of recruit Adams, eye-balled him up, and down, and bellowed a question. "Did you shine those boots this morning, Ree-cruit?"

"Yes Sir!" came Adams' reply.

"What did you use? A chocolate bar?" he demanded.

"No Sir!" Adams replied.

"Extra duty for dirty boots, Ree-cruit!" ordered Drill Sgt. Baker in a thundering voice.

The Drill Sgt. continued down the ranks, barking orders at Bagwell, Cadman, Coats, Colman, and others, handing out extra duty for deficiencies.

Stopping in front of Recruit Herman, he asked, "Did you shave this morning, Ree-cruit?"

"Yes Sir," Herman replied.

"Looks like you're growing a vegetable garden there! What did you use, a fork? Ree-cruit?"

"No Sir!" Herman replied.

"Extra duty for not shavin' Ree-cruit!" Drill Sgt. Baker ordered.

And so the inspection progressed, until the entire platoon had been inspected.

Sgt. Baker then moved front and center of the platoon, who were still standing at attention. And gave a lengthy commentary on how to get along in the United States Army.

"Aw-right, you Ree-cruits, if you wanna' get along in this man's Army; you'll either shape-up, or ship out! There's only *two ways* to do things, and that's *the wrong way*, and *the Army way!*"

"This winds up the inspection, We're gonna' go out to the firing range, and you're gonna' learn how to use the best friend a soldier ever has, the 30 Caliber, M-1 Rifle. Fall out! And Mount up!" the Sgt. ordered in a demanding voice.

The recruits loaded up, or "mounted up" as the Sgt. had ordered into a convoy of two waiting 6x6, 2 ½ ton trucks, and were transported to the firing range, where they were to spend the next two days, qualifying with their 'friend,' the M-1 Rifle.

The days were filled with diverse, and multiple activities, causing them to seemingly literally fly by. Time had passed so quickly that many of the recruits were looking forward to graduating from basic training, to become journeymen Army Private Infantrymen.

Graduation meant they would no longer be restricted to quarters, and would be assigned to Infantry Units. The best news to all, was that they would receive a furlough equal to two and a half days for every month of active duty, plus half a day for each weekend, meaning a fourteen-day furlough. Many of the recruits were already making plans as to where they were going, and what they were going to be doing on their leave after basic training.

Phil knew exactly what he was going to be doing. He was going home, catch up on sleep, and do absolutely nothing. He had heard from his sister that Jud had asked his Mother to marry him. He was glad for this and hoped his Mother would accept Jud's proposal. He was not aware his Mother had purposely withheld accepting Jud's proposal until she talked with him and received his opinion.

Finally, the much talked about, and much waited for day arrived. The recruits stood their last inspection in ranks, had a final inspection in quarters, prior to graduation, attended graduation, and completed basic training by "processing out."

The "processing out" was the reversal of "processing in." The M-1 Rifle, and all issued gear, except the fatigue, and dress uniform, (which the recruits had been obligated to buy), had to be turned in to Quartermaster Supply.

The graduates whose names had been called for "tentative shipping over", meaning going overseas, had to take another series of vaccinations. Phil was relieved his name had not been called from the list. He realized, since the list was "tentative", his name could still be added, to ship over with others, who had been ordered, after a fourteen-day leave, to be overseas troop replacements.

To kill time waiting for authorized furlough passes to be issued Phil, Clark, and some others, were walking around the base and passed the induction receiving center. They were pleased to see a new group of draftees being loaded into a 6x6, 2 ½ ton Army truck. Several of the graduates Phil and Clark were with got so bold, as to move close to the new arrivals, and taunt them with good-natured kidding saying, "You'll be sorry!

"Keep your eyes open and your mouth shut," another yelled out.

Still another cried out, "Don't volunteer for anything!"

The kidding went on until all the newly arrived draftees had been "mounted up" into the truck and driven away. Sitting in the back of the truck, the draftees responded by waving, and smiling, not sure, whether to take the advice offered seriously, and unaware of what was in store for them in the weeks ahead.

With more time to kill, before receiving their passes, Phil and Clark decided to take in a Disney movie being shown at a base theater. When they left the theater, night was beginning to set in.

They went back to the CO's (Commanding Officer) office, and received their "Official Passes" from the Company Clerk.

They called, and shared a cab, to the train depot. Since luggage had already been checked when they bought their tickets, it was just a matter of waiting for their train to arrive. They checked with the ticket office, to confirm the time of their trains' arrival, since they were traveling in opposite directions. While waiting they decided to wait in the train station café where, at the same time, they enjoyed a sandwich and a cup of coffee.

"What time does your train arrive, Phil?" Clark asked. "At 19:00 Hours. What about yours?" Phil asked.

"The ticket agent said it would be here by 21:00 Hours," Clark answered.

"You'll have to buy a book to read while you wait," Phil suggested.

"I'll have to do something," Clark replied.

The sandwich orders arrive and their conversation momentarily ended while eating.

By the time they finished eating, and drinking a second cup of coffee, it was 18:30 Hours. Walking from the café they heard the whistling sound of the arriving train blow once, twice, three times, breaking the silence, with each blast sounding closer.

Standing on the platform adjacent to the tracks they head a brakeman call out, "There she comes; right on time!"

The small train depot trembled when the train pulled abreast of the loading platform and shuddered to a stop.

"Well, Phil, you'll soon be on your way. I would like to tell you I have enjoyed knowing you, and becoming your friend. I hope we see each other again," Clark said.

"Likewise, Clark. I too have enjoyed your friendship, and who knows? Maybe we will meet again. Like they say, 'It's a small world.'"

Handing Phil a scribbled note Clark said, "Here's my home address, Phil. You can write to me there and my Mother will see that I get it. After the first letter, we will probably have a permanent military address."

In the background they could hear the Porter calling, "All Aboard! All Aboard!"

Phil replied, "Thanks, Clark. I hope we can stay in touch. Good luck to you, and God Bless," Phil said as they shook hands and said good-bye.

"So long. Soldier," Clark said, giving Phil a mock salute.

At 7 AM the following day the train stopped forty miles from Phil's home town. He had not written or notified his mother the day of his arrival because he wanted to surprise her. He decided to call and tell her what time he would arriving to have his brother pick him up at the train station.

Stepping from the train he walked the short distance across the platform to a phone booth. His Mother answered the phone. "Hello, Mother, how are you?" Phil spoke into the receiver.

At first his mother didn't recognize his voice. "Who is this?" she asked.

"Guess who?" Phil replied, teasing her.

Then hearing his now familiar voice she recognized him and said, "Oh, Phil, is it really you?"

"In the flesh," he answered.

"Where are you, Son?' she asked.

"About an hour from home. Will you have Mark meet me, and pick me up, at the train station around 7:30, please?" he replied and requested.

"Yes. I sure will, Son. Oh, I'm so excited to see you! Don't worry. We'll be there to meet you," she assured him.

"Thanks, Mom. I'll see you soon. Bye for now," he said, hanging up the phone.

It was close to eight o'clock when the train pulled into the depot in Phil's home town. Getting off the train, he stood for a few minutes, taking in all the familiar sights around him. He saw his mother, brother, Mark, and sister, Mary, waiting for him. Grabbing his duffle bag, he ran to meet them. His mother was exceedingly glad to see him. She embraced him tightly, and shed tears of joy.

Arriving in the city and driving up Main Street on the way home he became aware of the sights he had seen a hundred times, all so familiar, yet at the same time seemed strange as he noticed details of sights he had seen a thousand times. In his mind he reasoned, you can look at building, landscapes, and scenery, time after time, and never really see them, until you are away from them. And then, when you return, you appreciate the detail, and can really see them for the very first time.

After dinner that evening, Phil and Jud watched some favorite programs on the television. Later when Jud had gone home and the family was preparing for bed, Phil's mother told him she wanted to talk with him. Putting on a robe he went to the kitchen where his mother was brewing a pot of coffee.

After the coffee brewed his mother placed a cup of hot, black coffee, and a plate of brownies in front of him. They enjoyed the coffee and brownies before engaging in conversation.

"What's on your mind, Mom?" Phil asked.

"Well Phil, as you might have guessed, Jud has asked me to marry him. I was wondering what your thoughts are on this?" She asked.

"Mom, I can't tell you what to do, or not to do. I will tell you what I think, and what I would do."

Phil explained his thinking by saying, "In the first place, I believe it is God's will that men and women should be united in holy matrimony. Since you have been married, you, and only you, know whether you want to remarry or stay single. Personally, I would remarry. I think Jud is a real nice person, even though I don't know him very well. I believe he would make you a good husband. One question I would ask you. Is he a Christian?"

"Yes. Yes, he is. He has taken me to church, ever since I have known him." she answered.

"Then, I believe, if I were you, I would marry him," Phil explained his thinking.

"Thank you so much, Son. You have eased my mind, to know that you feel as I do," she replied, smiling at her son.

Phil was pleased his Mother valued his approval, or at least his opinion, regarding her marriage to Jud, and had wanted to talk to him to see if he agreed with her thinking, before accepting Jud's proposal.

During the short time he would be home, he had much to do. He wanted to go to his former employer, at the plant where he had worked, to visit with former co-workers, especially Harve. He also wanted to spend some time with Evelyn.

The first three days at home he did very little. Mostly catching up on sleep. He slept undisturbed to a late morning hour, then got up to face the rest of the day, to relax, visit with friends, both in person, and by phone.

Although he did not show alarm to his mother, relatives, and friends, he became increasingly concerned over the situation brewing in North Korea. He knew, if worse came to worst, he would be one of the first to be called up for military duty.

It appeared Phil was not alone in his concern. As a result of the continued raids by North Korea on the United States Military, and allies at the 38th Parallel border, fear was being aroused across the nation; fear of war.

Trying to empty his mind about threat of war, Phil called Evelyn on Saturday. He asked for, and received consent to see her.

"Oh, Phil. I'm so glad you came to see me. I heard you were home, and was hoping you would stop by," she told him.

"You know I wouldn't leave without seeing you, Ev," he answered.

"How's the Army?" she asked.

"Still there, or it was, when I left," Phil teased.

"Quit your kidding. You know what I mean," she chided him

"Yeah. I know what you mean. You mean how's the KP Duty, the floor scrubbing, latrine duty, and all that," he continued joking with her.

"No, silly. I mean, how do you like it?" Evelyn responded.

"It's ok for variety, and as they say, 'variety is the spice of life, if you want to be well-seasoned.' No. Seriously, I got along good," Phil answered, becoming more serious.

"You're looking good. You look like you have gained weight," She commented.

"I have, although I'll never know how, on the food they gave us to eat," he said. Pausing for a few seconds he continued. "I wanted to ask you to go to church with me this Sunday."

"I'd love to. I'm sure Mother won't object," she replied.

"Not to your church this time. Ev. To my Mother's church. I want to spend as much time as possible with her," Phil explained.

"I'm sure I can go. Do they hold the service at the same time?" she asked.

"Yes. It's at 11 o'clock. I'll pick you up about 10:30. I have a lot to do in such a short time. So I'll see you tomorrow," he said, kissing her lightly on the cheek.

"Ok, Phil, see you tomorrow," she acknowledged.

Saturday evening many relatives came to Phil's mother's home to have a potluck dinner to visit, wish him well, and to say good-bye with God's blessings.

Phil picked up Evelyn for church on Sunday. He decided to wear his uniform to let those know, who didn't know already, he was now a soldier in the United States Army.

Arriving at church, they found Phil's family waiting in their car, so they could all enter, and be seated together. Evelyn had met Phil's mother, and family before. They exchanged cordial and friendly greetings. She offered her hand when Phil introduced her to Jud and said, "I'm pleased to meet you, Mr. Matthews."

"It's my pleasure. I've heard many good thing about you," Jud replied.

Walking into the church they were seated by the ushers. The order of service progressed to announcements. Phil listened, without really hearing, until he heard the reverend mention the family name, and then heard the Pastor say, "I have a very special announcement this morning about the Kingsley family. We are happy to see Phil Kingsley in our service. Phil recently became a member of the military. Phil, we wish you a lot of success, with God's Blessing while serving in the Army."

Phil's mind flashed back to another time, when the reverend had not been so happy to see him. The night he had been caught him drinking beer in the church parking lot. With a smile Phil was glad to recall, since his conversion, this was a part of the past, and now history.

The reverend was not finished. He continued with, "I have another very special announcement. I'm also pleased to report, Mrs. Nora Kingsley has informed me, that she and Jud Matthews, a member of our Church, will be married this coming week. We are so happy to learn of this soon to be wedding. Congratulations are in order for this fine Christian couple."

The announcement was not as much a surprise to Phil, as it was to everyone else. In his mind he was thinking. "Boy! When Mom makes up her mind, she doesn't let any grass grow under her feet!" He caught his mother's eye and smiled 'Congratulations!'

The church service ended, and the benedictory prayer was given, signaling the dismissal of the congregation.

Congregants rushed to congratulate Nora Kingsley and Jud Matthews on their upcoming wedding, with handshakes, back slaps and little old, tear-eyed ladies, all anxious to wish them happiness.

Phil and Evelyn broke away from the crowd of well-wishers and walked to the car. Once inside the car Evelyn asked, "Why didn't you tell me, Phil?"

"This is the first of I knew of it," Phil answered.

"I'm so happy for them. Isn't it sweet of your mother to get married while you are home?"

"Yes. Yes, it is. I have a wonderful mother, he answered.

"Why don't you stay and have lunch with us?" she invited

"I'd love to, Eve, but I better spend as much of my remaining time as I can, with my family. If I don't get a chance to see you again, before my leave is up, please get my address from my Mother and write to me," he requested.

"I sure will, Phil. And if I don't see you again for a while, my prayers, and God's blessing go with you. Take care of yourself," she said, turning and giving him a gentle kiss.

"Thank you. Bye for now," he replied, giving her a hug. Without looking back, he drove away.

Phil's mother and Jud were already home when he arrived. He could smell his favorite dish cooking when he walked into the kitchen.

Grinning, he said, "Hi Mom. What's for lunch?"

"As if you didn't already know. Chicken 'n Dumplings, of course, your favorite," she replied giving him a hug.

Phil went into the bedroom, changed from his uniform to a pair of jeans and sport shirt, and came back out into the living room to join Jud, who was reading the Sunday paper. His little sister, Sharon, came to sit on her brother's lap. Phil read the comic pages to her. She was sound asleep by the time lunch was ready.

Joining the family, Phil enjoyed the best meal he had eaten, since before leaving for the military.

His mother and Jud sat at the table and made plans for the wedding. They deiced to have the ceremony in the church parlor, with only a few friends, and family attending. Phil was to be the best man, and his mother's best friend Nelda Sanderson, was to be the matron of honor. In a very quick time, plans were set. The wedding date would be Wednesday, June 28th. At 7:30 PM, just three days away.

The afternoon seemed to fly by. It seemed to Phil like they had just gotten up from the lunch table when his mother started setting out sandwiches, coffee, lemonade, and cake for a light evening snack. Jud, who was in the habit of watching the news and weather report, turned on the television, so they could watch while snacking. The day was June 25th, the year 1950.

The unwelcome voice of a news announcer filled the room, and shocked the listener. "Due to North Korea invading South Korea with a formidable force of tanks, artillery, and troops, against the Free Republic of South Korea at 4:00 AM this morning, the Secretary General, of the United Nations, has called a meeting with the President, Secretary of Defense, and the Security Council, at Lake Success, New York."

"The Security Council is requesting action be taken, demanding the North Korean Republic to immediately withdraw its troops border of the 38th Parallel". The Secretary of Defense, on orders of the President, states that, if the North Korean Republic does not comply with the demand, and troops are not immediately withdrawn, an inevitable police action will begin, to force the North Korean Republic Army North of the 38th Parallel. This is a breaking news story. This is an ongoing story. This station will keep you informed on further developments."

The impact, of what he had just heard, was lost on Phil, while he was trying to process what had just been announced. The eyes of his relatives turned to him, as he sat in stunned silence.

All were aware of the consequences that a world crisis police action, would have on him concerning his military status.

CHAPTER 18

Away to War

The next day, Monday, Phil decided to go to his former place of employment. Arriving at lunch time, and going to the lunch room, he was able to visit a few former co-workers. Most were pleased to see him. Going from the lunch room to the cafeteria, he was able to locate Harve, who having finished lunch, was enjoying a cup of coffee.

"Well, well. How's the big soldier boy?" he greeted Phil with an inquisitive voice.

"Good, Harve. Good. And yourself?" Phil answered.

"Doin' ok," replied Harve.

"It's good to see you, again. I'm on leave for a few more days, and I wanted to come by and see you," Phil explained.

"Glad you could make it, Phil," he replied.

"Have you heard the latest news about North Korea? And if so, what do you think about it, Harve?' Phil asked.

"Aw. Hell. It's just a bunch of hot heads acting out. Nothin' will come of it," he answered.

"You don't think so, huh?' Phil asked.

"Well. Ya' never know. But I don't think so," he replied.

"Didn't you tell me you belonged to an Infantry National Guard Battalion? If a Police Action, or war comes, how do you think that will affect you?" Phil asked a double question.

"Yeah. I belong to an active Infantry National Guard Unit. As a matter of fact, we have been placed on 'Ready Alert,' for a recall, just in case. But like I said, I think the whole thing will blow over," Harve said, sounding like he needed to convince himself, more than Phil.

"I sure hope you're right, but I don't have the feeling that you are," Phil replied.

"Well, I gotta' get back to work. Come around at quitting time and I'll buy ya a … milk shake, he said grinning devilishly. He had started to say drink, but suddenly remembered, Phil no longer was a drinker.

"No. I have many things to do before my leave is up. If I don't get a chance to see you again for a while, I'll try to drop you a line from time to time," Phil promised.

"Ok. Do that, Phil. Who knows? Maybe I'll see ya' in Korea!" Harve said, with a burst of laughter. They shook hands and parted. Little did Harve know, with that parting remark, he was sealing his own fate.

That Monday evening, Phil's family had invited their pastor to their home to discuss the wedding. They enjoyed the company of the pastor and wife.

On Tuesday, Phil was anxiously watching the news, catching up on current events regarding North Korea. The voice of the news anchor broke in saying, "This is breaking News! It is being reported, The Republic of North Korea has rejected the Secretary General of the United Nations' demand to withdraw its troops north of the 38th Parallel."

"As a result, the Secretary of Defense, by orders of the President, has authorized the commitment of air, and sea support for the South Korea Army with a police action that will begin immediately, defending the border of the 38th Parallel.

Phil was experiencing mixed emotions. Being much in prayer, during the trying days, knowing his own life might be in danger. He was also praying God's will, in the matter, would be done. His belief, as a new believer, instead of becoming doubtful and weaker, was in fact, becoming stronger, maturing as a Christian, on the pathway of life, in his journey of faith.

Most of Wednesday was taken with activates related to the wedding. His mother had him busy helping her to clean, and straighten the house, because the reception was to be held there. He didn't mind helping, since it took his mind off of what part, or role, he might play, if called to war in Korea. He was glad for having something to do, so he didn't have time to think.

Having finished helping his mother, he began to pack for his return to the base for re-assignment. He found it difficult to maintain a pleasant attitude during the remainder of his leave. He felt caught, between being concerned for his own welfare, and at the same time, wanting to share in his mother's happiness.

He felt tempted to go buy a pack of cigarettes, and smoke, to relieve his nervous tension, or to have a beer or two, and once again, participate in activities that was now a part of his past. To overcome temptation, he reminded himself, that the eyes of his small world was watching, waiting, hoping, and in some cases praying, he would step down from the pedestal, he had seemingly placed himself on, when he turned from his sin-filled life.

His mother and Jud's wedding was beautifully performed by the pastor. As best man, Phil had been so nervous he almost dropped the ring when handing it to Jud, but luckily, he didn't.

The group of immediate relatives and close friends hurriedly left and proceeded to the Kingsley home and upon arriving wrote "Just Married" on Jud's car rear window, and attached numerous crepe paper streamers. The reception lasted well into the late evening. Phil was exhausted when the last of the guests left.

The newlyweds decided to delay their honeymoon until after Phil's leave was over, just two days away.

Phil learned his mother made a wise choice in choosing Jud Matthews for a husband. Some of Jud's history increased his respect for him. He learned Jud became a widower in the winter of 1940, and he had two adult children; a girl and a boy, who both were married with their own families. During WWII, he become semi-wealthy working in the ship yard and through smart investing in real estate. Phil's mind was eased in knowing his mother now no longer needed to be concerned about security, and could fully enjoy the remaining years of life.

Friday was the day Phil had to travel to his new assigned base for deployment. Time had passed so quickly he hardly had time to realize his leave was over. His mind was filled with a sense of ambivalence about the world situation, the loss of life, possibly his own, and at the same time, much respect for the firm stand the United States had taken regarding North Korea. He was both anxious, and reluctant, to go to his new duty station for assignment and deployment.

Sadness surrounded his leaving because of tears shed by his mother and sisters. Saying good-bye to all, he prided himself on being dry-eyed, and felt a warm sense of contentment witnessing his mother and Jud together, in their new found happiness.

Waving a final good-bye through the window, to family and friends, who had accompanied him to the train depot, he settled into the seat trying to find a comfortable position. His family stood and waved after the train as it pulled out of the station.

Phil reported to his new duty session on the east coast, and was shown to his quarters. Before having opportunity to square away his gear, a whistle sounded, followed up by a voice yelling, "Fall in for roll call!"

Standing at attention, a heavy-set, middle-aged sergeant named Doyle commanded them to stand "At ease!" He then began speaking with a heavy accent giving an announcement.

"Aw' right youse' guys, gimmie your ears. As some of youse' know, some of youse' guys are fresh outa' boot camp. It's the plan of the CO (Commanding Officer) to assign youse' to different T.O. & E. (Table of Organization and Equipment), positions, and to place all of youse' in different companies of the battalion. But there have been some changes. All of youse' guys, whose names I call, are scheduled for overseas shipment with transfer to another infantry battalion. When I call your name sound off, and take one step forward," he ordered.

The sergeant started down the list calling out the names of the ones whose overseas orders had been cut. In alphabetical order, the sergeant called out the names. And so it went, down the shipping order list.

"Archer, Dean,"

"Here Sir,"

"Burns, Sam,"

"Here Sir,"

"Cory, Jerold,"

"Here Sir,"

"Davis, Clyde,"

"English, James,"

"Here Sir,"

"Franklin, Joseph,"

"Here Sir,"

"Love, Carl,"

"Here Sir,"

Phil listened until he heard the name "Love" and then breathed a sigh of relief. The sergeant had passed over the "K's" on the list. Suddenly, the sergeant stopped calling names. He looked at the list with a puzzled look. He grunted, and then said, "I missed a coupla' names under the "K's". Sound off when I call your name.

"Kranston, Michael,"

"Here Sir,"

"Kingsley, Phillip,"

"Here Sir," Phil answered and stepped forward.

Phil's mind was racing a mile a minute as he listened to the sergeant's monotonous voice calling out other names. He was thinking, "Well, Phil, you lucked out again."

Finishing roll call, the sergeant said, "Aw' right, ever' body's name I called, report to the Officer of the Day in the Company Orderly Room, for your shipping out orders. The rest of youse' stay in this area, and God help you, if I catch any of youse' gold brickin,' (goofing off). Fall Out!" he ordered, and dismissed the troops.

Phil had one consolation. He was glad he was not going to be assigned to the infantry company Sgt. Doyle was in charge of.

Entering the Orderly Room, he reported to a 2nd Lieutenant John, who was the Officer of the Day.

Standing at attention, and saluting, he said, "Private Kingsley, Phillip E., 28982552, reporting as directed, Sir."

"At ease, Kingsley," the Lieutenant ordered, returning the salute. "Here are your Orders. You are to report immediately to Rifle Company A, of the 45th Infantry Division. I'll give you a little background. The 45th is an Army National Guard Division that has just been activated. Since your basic training was at infantry level, you shouldn't have any difficulty fitting in. The entire division is on Stand-by Alert Duty, waiting for orders to ship over. Any other questions you have will be answered when you read your orders. Good luck to you. Be safe out there, soldier," the Lieutenant challenged, and cautioned.

"Thank you, Sir," Phil replied, snapped to attention, and gave the best salute he had given since joining the Army.

Phil reported to Captain Miller, the Commander of A Company, 45th Army National Guard Infantry Division, and was assigned to Company A. The duty was unlike Phil had ever experienced. Rules and regulations had seemingly been relaxed, while the troops waited orders to be shipped overseas.

Soldiers came and went at will. There was no reveille, only retreat for roll call. The rumor was, Guard Units were going to Korea as replacement Troops, and would see combat. After combat, as the police action as it was being referred to, progressed toward Peace Talks, which had started, two Divisions, the 40th and the 45th, would be re-assigned to Japan, where they would train and serve as the defensive garrison.

The first day, preparing for retreat, Phil had opportunity to meet some of the other soldiers. Forbes, an engineer in civilian life; Hanson, an over the road truck driver; Griffin, a police officer; Carpenter, a sales representative for a pharmaceutical company, and others, who Phil was destined to meet and share military life with.

Phil had just finished 'spit shining' his boots when the whistle sounded for retreat and roll call.

There was something vaguely familiar about the sergeant standing front and center before the platoon. Even his voice sounded familiar when he ordered, "Fall in; Dress Right, Dress." (Meaning soldiers bring up their left arms, parallel to the ground. At the same time, all members of the formation snap their heads so they are facing right, followed by command of, "Normal interval; Ten hut", soldiers coming to attention).

The sergeant ordered, "Parade Rest." (A position assumed by a soldier in which the feet are 12 inches apart, and the hands are clasped behind the back, and the head is held motionless, facing forward). The Sergeant then begin the roll call.

Although Phil only glimpsed the platoon sergeant, he was wondering where he had seen him before. The sergeant held a clipboard and begin to call roll. Running quickly down the list making notations beside the name he had called as to present or absent.

"Kingsley, Phillip,"

"Here Sir," Phil responded.

The sergeant paused after calling Phil's name, and called the name again, "Kingsley, Phillip,"

"Here Sir," Phil repeated his presence.

Finishing roll call, the sergeant executed an about face, reported "all present and accounted for," to the First Sergeant, and stood at attention.

The sergeant was also wondering if this was the Phillip Kingsley he knew. His old drinkin' buddy. The convert. The one who had gotten' religion. He would soon find out.

The military reports went through the chain of command from the Division Commander down to "A" Alpha Company; "B" Bravo Company; "C" Charlie Company, and others reporting "All present and accounted for." After which the Division Commander ordered, "Bring your Companies to Parade Rest."

All Company Commanders, almost in unison, ordered their company to "Parade Rest!"

The distant strains of bugle music sounded as retreat was played.

The Division Commander snapped to attention, and called the division to "Ten Hut!" (Attention) and then to "Present Arms." The troops held the position of, at attention, presenting arms, until the command of "Order Arms," was given. The Division Commander than ordered all Company Commanders, "Front and Center!'

The troops stood at attention for another five minutes while the Division Commander briefed the Company Commanders. After briefing the Company Commanders resumed their position in front of their Companies.

The Division Commander then ordered Company Commanders, "Brief your Companies!"

Salutes were exchange, and the Division Commander disappeared. Company Commanders ordered their Companies to "Parade Rest" and begin the briefing.

"A" Company Commander, Captain Miller, paused for a few seconds, and then started to speak, "Listen up! We have just been notified we will be shipping out tomorrow at 16:30 Hours. Be sure to secure your gear and be ready to roll. Have a good night tonight on liberty. Get a good night's rest and sleep. And above all, stay sober," Captain Miller said, with a grin, called the company to "Ten Hut!" He exchanged salutes with the First Sergeant, and turned the company over to him, and disappeared.

The First Sergeant challenged the troops, "You heard what the CO said. Have a good time tonight, stay sober, and by all means, be here with all your gear at 16:30 Hours for roll call and shipping over tomorrow afternoon.

The Sergeant then ordered the company to be "Dismissed!"

Phil had just reached the door to his barracks when he heard someone call his name, "Kingsley, hold up!" the voice instructed. He turned toward the sound of the voice and recognized the Platoon Sergeant who had taken roll call on his arrival. Phil wondered what to expect.

The sergeant came to a halt before Phil. Taking off his fatigue service cap, to reveal a military cut of black hair. "It's me, Phil, Harve, your old drinkin' buddy!" Harve exclaimed.

"Well! I'll be darned!" Phil responded. "It sure is a small world! I didn't recognize you in uniform, Harve. It's good to see you!" Phil, continued his greeting, shaking Harve's hand.

"Yeah. I didn't recognize you either in ranks when I called roll. But when I saw your name, I didn't think there could be two Kingsley's, with the name of Phillip. Man, I'm glad you were assigned to the Army Guard and landed in my unit. We can really have a ball together tonight."

"It depends on what you call a 'ball' " Phil replied laughing.

"I know these two girls I've met since I've been here. They are cool. I can set 'em up for a double date tonight, and we can really have a blast," Harve continued.

"I don't mind having some female companionship, but I plan on staying sober." Phil reminded Harve.

"Sure. Sure. You and Peggy can play tiddlywinks, while Carol and I drink up a storm. As a matter of fact, you can look out for me," Harve said with a laugh.

"As if you need it," Phil replied joining in the laughter.

Harve went to a public phone booth and called Carol to make date arrangements. Then he and Phil walked to the service club to have sandwiches and coffee. After which, they went to the guard entrance, to wait for the girls to arrive and pick them up.

They didn't have to wait long. Just outside the guard gate Phil noticed two females sitting in a Cadillac Eldorado. He started to say something to Harve when he noticed Harve heading directly toward the Cadillac.

Phil followed Harve to the Cadillac. Harve greeted the driver, "Hi'ya, Carol, baby! I want you to meet a buddy I knew in civilian life. Carol, this is Phil, Phil Kingsley. Phil this is Carol," Harve introduced them. They exchanged greetings. Then Carol introduced Phil to her friend Peggy. "Peggy, this is Harve's friend, Phil. Phil, this is Peggy."

Peggy said, "Hi, Handsome," as she moved the seat back for him to get into the back seat. Phil noticed the smell of liquor on Carol's breath when he entered the car.

Once both were in the car, Carol grabbed Harve in a hug and placed a big kiss full on his lips. Prior to her moving toward Harve she had lounged behind the wheel of the Cadillac with her tight dress hugging her body and exposing her lower extremities well above the knee. That which was not exposed was sharply revealed by her tight dress.

Sitting in the back seat, Peggy moved close to Phil and reached for his hand. Telling him how nice it was, to meet him.

Carol broke from the hug with Harve, started the engine, and quickly drove the Cadillac past seventy miles per hour, in a forty-five mile an hour posted speed limit zone. Phil and Peggy discussed everything from the weather to the books they had read on the way to their apartment house destination.

Carol pulled into a space clearly marked "No Parking at Any Time" and the four climbed from the car. It was obvious to Phil that Carol apparently was wealthy. He had not been impressed by either the car or the diamonds she wore on her fingers, or around her neck. But as they entered the apartment, he was aware of the expensive furnishings, and realized that to live in this luxury apartment one had to have a substantial income, or a heavy financial resource.

Entering a self-service elevator, they ascended to a pent-house apartment capturing an ocean view, and in the background, the twinkling bright lights of the city.

Carol walked into a small bar and asked, "What would every one like to drink?"

"Seven up, for me," Phil said.

"Seven-up, and seven-up, it will be," she replied. At first Phil thought she was going to make some smart remark, but she didn't.

Peggy chose a "Screwdriver" (Vodka and Orange Juice).

By the second drink Peggy took Phil by the hand and said, "Let's go out on the patio."

"Sounds like a plan," Phil replied, following her to the patio.

They were barely out of the room before Harve and Carol were in a lovers embrace. The sound of knocking over of furniture and labored breathing left little to the imagination as to what was happening, and as to what kind of girl Carol was.

Phil was wondering just what kind of girl Peggy was as they sat close together in the semi-darkness on the patio. She appeared to be unmoved by the sounds from inside, and was even oblivious to them while they chatted about the military, how long Phil had been in, and what he planned to do when he got out.

Phil had noticed a small theater when they arrived and walked through the lobby. A note in the elevator announced a current movie was scheduled to play, and repeat playing, until midnight, and was provided for resident entertainment.

Soon Harve stood in the doorway of the patio and asked, "Anybody ready for another drink?"

"None for me," Phil replied.

"No. I don't think so. Thanks anyway Harve," Peggy answered.

"Party poopers," Harve said in a disgusted voice, and headed back to the bar for a refill.

"I noticed a theater when we came in playing a current movie until midnight. Let's go to a movie, Peggy," Phil suggested.

"Ok, lead the way," Peggy said, accepting the invitation.

Phil helped Peggy put on her white, short coat and they left the room for the theater.

At 15:40 Hours the next day, the troops broke from ranks, after roll call, to begin loading on to a U.S. Army Transport Ship lying in the harbor, waiting to take them to Korea. Phil had not seen Harve since the night before. In fact, the ranking non-com (Non-Commissioned Officer), Corporal Swain had taken his place in front of the troops for roll call.

Having loaded on the U.S. Army Transport Ship Phil stood on deck looking out across the harbor waiting for the ship to get underway. He heard a voice at his elbow.

"A fine friend you turned out to be. I fix you up with a nice chick and all the free booze you can drink and you run out on me," Harve said.

Phil turned to Harve just as the engines of the ship roared to life, and the ship lurched backward. Harve grabbed the rail with both hands, and turned a shade paler than he already was. Phil could see that his friend was suffering from a hangover.

"I told you Harve that I was going to stay sober. The type of activities you enjoyed last night was once a part of my life, but not anymore," Phil replied.

"Oh, brother! Aren't you the holy one?" Harve countered.

By this time the ship had cleared the harbor and had headed out to sea. It began to rise and fall with the swell of the ocean. With each rise and fall of the waves, Harve's complexion changed from a pasty white to deep red.

"At least, I'm not suffering from a hangover, "Phil said, with a trace of laughter in his voice

Harve gave no reply, as he hung his head over the rail, gagged several times before vomiting. In his mind he was promising himself, this was the last time, he was going to get so falling down drunk. Deep down inside he was beginning to respect Phil for his total abstinence, and inwardly wished he had the will power, to resist the things he knew were not good for him.

Phil steered Harve to the sleeping quarter of the ship, found a bunk for Harve to sack out on and sleep off his hangover.

Phil returned to the deck and walked aft of the ship. Standing for several minutes, with his foot on the lower rail, he watched the ship's wake as it churned and stirred the waters to a foamy white.

His thoughts tuned to the times he, too, had suffered from hangovers. He recalled, at the time, he thought he was having the time of his life. He realized now, there was more to life than drinking, partying, and participating in sexual activity, which the world considered a "good time."

He stood for a long time on the open deck, gazing at the vastness around him. It seemed like the ship would never stop tossing, rolling, rising, and falling with the turbulence of the waves.

The coolness of the evening became chilling. The sun had set, and nightfall was being pursued by darkness. He decided to go below and write a letter home.

After what seemed like an eternity to Phil the ship was finally preparing to anchor in the harbor of the seacoast town of Fukuoka, Japan. Pulling into the harbor, many of the troops lined the rail. It seemed like hundreds of Japanese residents were waiting on the pier. Their faces broke into grins and smiles as they waved to the American troops as they were recognized and welcomed. They were greeted with happiness, good will, and shouts of joy.

The Japanese people were very glad to see the "Yanks," shown by the greeting they received.

CHAPTER 19

Date with Destiny

Since the troops were waiting for orders, to be combat replacements, and in the field reinforcement for ground troop infantry units, it was necessary to use the ship for temporary quarters. While waiting, some of the troops felt they had been led on a wild goose chase, and ultimately would be receiving orders to return to home base without disembarking.

The Russian Foreign Minister, Gromyko, was "mouthing off", demanding "immediate evacuation of all US Military Troops from South Korea". In reply to the demand, the United Nations was firmly resolved to unite a commanding force consisting of a number of nation allies with Air, Ground, and Sea support, by order of the United States President, under direction of Commanding General, Dwayne McInerny, to put down the act of aggression.

Aboard ship there was a sense of anxiety and frustration. The longer the wait, the greater the anxiety. The overwhelming cloud of the "unknown" shrouded by not knowing what to expect increased frustration. Listening to news report led some to believe they were ready to go home. The next news bulletin assured them, and the world, that the United States Military intended to end the Communist invasion against South Korea.

Observing the troops to be restless and uneasy waiting the "call to duty", the Commanding Officer passed down the word through the chain of command that the troops could have A VOCO Pass (Verbal Order of Commanding General), (VOCO = Order of Commanding Officer), and, consequently a "night on the town".

When Harve heard this good news, he all but shouted for joy.

"Holy Moley, Phil. We can find us some oriental women and have us a tall ball," he exclaimed.

"Don't kid yourself, Harve, these "oriental women," as you call them, wouldn't even give you the time of day," Phil answered.

"Oh, yeah! Wanna bet? I bet you I can have one of these babes by 18:00 Hours!" Harve challenged.

"Ok. If you say you can, then you can," Phil teasingly replied.

"You won't bet me, then?" Harve asked.

"No, 'fraid not," Phil answered.

Phil, Harve, and several others walked off the ship into the streets of Fukuoka, Japan. They decided to do a little sight-seeing before trying to enjoy any entertainment the town had to offer.

Almost immediately they were approached by a young Japanese man pulling a rickshaw. In broken English he solicited their transportation business.

"Yankee ride? See Geisha girls? Have good time, huh?" he invited. They were amused by his pleading cries, but refused his offer, wanting to walk instead.

The litter of paper and debris cluttering the streets, lined with crowds of people, including what appeared to be homeless beggars, hands out for denotations, reminded them of the skid-rows of major cities in the United States. They were amazed at the seeming lack of cleanliness, and had expected something much different.

The crowded and conglomerated windows of store fronts held their interest as they stared fascinated at the many trinkets and curios the window displayed. Tired of window shopping they continued to walk down the crowded street. Suddenly, Phil felt a tugging at his elbow. He turned to see a sallow faced man with beady eyes and yellow stained teeth.

"Yanks want good time, huh? Hosho got just right place. Only ten American dollars for pretty women, much drinks, and good time, huh?" he invited.

"What's all that jazz he is spouting, Phil?" Harve asked.

"He says, here's your chance to have one of those oriental babes you wanted," Phil answered.

"No, thanks. I'll do my own scouting, if you don't mind. There isn't any challenge to getting a women his way," Harve disgustedly replied.

Even as he spoke, his eyes were following the swinging hips of two young females who had just passed them while they stood on the street listening to the native.

Harve nudged Phil's arm and said, "Hey, Man, dig those two slick chicks. Check that rhythm section," he continued, while he intently gazed at the exaggerated walk of the two girls, who were well aware they were being noticed.

"Let's follow them," Harve suggested.

At first Phil was hesitant, but then decided it wouldn't hurt to just follow them, so he turned to Harve and said, "Alright, Romeo. It's your show. Lead the way."

They followed the girls for approximately two blocks before they turned into a doorway. Harve thought they had been ditched for a minute, until he saw the girls standing in the semi-darkness of the doorway to a restroom, with purses open, touching up make-up before entering the night club. They were obviously waiting for the soldiers to catch up to them.

When Phil and Harve approached the girls saw them, before opening the door and disappearing inside.

"What do you think is inside there, Harve?" Phil asked.

"Only one way to find out. Let's go inside," Harve answered.

They swung open the door and stood for several minutes while their eyes adjusted to the dimly lighted room, and then inspected the interior.

"It's a beer joint," Phil said.

"So it is. Do you see those babes?" Harve asked.

"Yes. They are over in the corner booth," Phil answered.

"That's them. And they are alone. Let's join them," Harve said.

"Ok, but remember. No booze for me," Phil reminded his friend.

"You can drink tea, for all I care," Harve assured him.

They crossed the room and stopped in front of the girl's booth. Harve asked, "Can we buy you ladies a drink?"

The one to whom Harve had spoken looked up, and replied in perfect English, with an Asian accent, "It would be a pleasure, Yanks. Be seated."

She slid across the seat making room for Harve and Phil. When they were seated the waitress was signaled and drinks were ordered; Japanese beer and tea for Phil. While waiting for drinks a brief silence was broken by Harve asking, "Where you ladies going tonight?"

"No plans," they replied almost in unison.

Phil decided to join the conversation by asking, "What are your names?"

He looked at their faces while waiting for the answer, and noticed they were heavily made up in cosmetics with powder and rouge accentuating their cheeks, and lips painted a bright red.

The girl sitting next to Harve answered Phil's question, "I'm Miayouko and this is Kiki," she said gesturing toward her friend. "Our nicknames are Mia and Ki," she answered.

Harve made the introduction of him and Phil saying, "I'm Harve, and this is Phil."

"It's nice to meet you," Phil said.

"Enough of this conversation. Now that we know each other, let's drink up with a toast," Harve suggested, raising his glass, and touching the others' glasses. "To a wonderful, enjoyable evening."

"Are all in agreement?" Harve asked, after the toast. All agreed they were.

And so the evening was spent, with round after round of drinks for the foursome.

Phil tried to keep the conversation light, so not to appear to be a "party pooper" as he slowly became tea logged.

When the bar was getting ready to close at 2:00 AM, Harve suggested they go out for a bite to eat.

Mia immediately suggested "Why don't we all go up to my, and Ki's apartment, and have something there?"

"Th'as a great idea," Harve thickly replied.

Walking to the exit they were greeted by a Japanese matron who spoke in Japanese, saying, "Gokuro Sama, gokuro Sama," bowing as they walked out into the early morning hour.

"What did she say to us, Mia?' Harve loudly asked.

"She was only thanking us for bringing them guests," Mia answered.

"Oh, is that all?" he murmured.

After a fifteen-minute walk they arrived at the girl's apartment. Entering the vestibule of the three-story structure, the girls walked toward a narrow hallway leading to a long, winding staircase.

"Which floor?" Harve asked.

"The top floor," Mia answered.

"Let's take the elevator," Harve suggested.

"There is no elevator," Mia answered.

"Oh crap!" Harve responded as he and the others begin staggering up the stairs.

All, except Phil, were tipsy from the long evening of drinking.

Arriving at the third floor, Ki unlocked the door and invited them in. Both Mia and Ki announced they were going to the kitchen and disappeared.

Phil seated himself on a sofa next to a bamboo end table. He picked up an old American magazine from the table and started thumbing through it.

Harve rummaged through a room divider that had been set up to resemble a bar trying to find something to drink.

Mia and Ki soon returned to the living room carrying a tray of tea and little rice cakes and egg rolls.

"No tea for me. Do you have anything else to drink, besides alcohol?" Phil asked.

"Sure we do. But let's have some food first. We can drink later.' Ki said.

Harve quickly ate several of the rice cakes and egg rolls, anxious to start having more to drink.

Phil and Ki ate some of the rice cakes and an egg roll. Suddenly, Ki grabbed Phil's hand and said, "Come on Phil. I'll show you my half of the apartment."

She led him into a short hallway which divided the apartment. A bedroom and private bath was located on each side of the hallway. Phil followed Ki into the spacious bedroom, where another room divider, similar to the one in the living room, projected out from the wall, filled with liquor; tall, skinny bottles, short, fat bottles, and bottles of various sizes lined the shelves of the room divider bar.

"How about a drink of good scotch, Phil," Ki asked.

"No, thanks. I don't drink," Phil replied.

Oh, come on. Just one little drink with me," she pleaded.

"No. Thank you. I don't drink," Phil repeated.

"Now look, Phil. I know you are trying to make an impression on your friend, by being a goody-goody boy. I won't tell him; no one will ever know," Ki insisted.

"No, thanks, Ki. I just don't drink anymore. Sure, I want to, but that's a part of my past," Phil explained.

"Oh, Come on Big Boy. Just one little drink with me," Ki continued to plead with Phil, putting her arm around his shoulders, putting his head up against her breast.

"You obviously don't take no for an answer, but I mean what I say, and say what I mean," Phil said more forcefully.

"You think about it for a few minutes, while I make myself more comfortable," Ki said and left the room.

Phil sat and pondered. He was torn between the desire to give in to temptation, and the will to resist. He suddenly remembered a verse of Scripture he had come across during his daily devotional readings, reminding him, "The spirit is willing, but the flesh is week." (Matthew 26:41).

He thought to himself, "How true; how very true."

His thoughts were interrupted by the opening and closing of the bathroom door. Ki walked toward him. She stood before him, dressed only in a silk negligee, with the top loosely open, revealing the fullness of her breasts.

"What did you decide?' she asked, teasing him, as she sat down on his lap.

"You make it awfully hard to say no," Phil replied.

"Then you'll have one?" Ki said, with a note of confidence in her voice. She got up from Phil's lap, "I have to get some ice from the kitchen. I'll be right back," she said before placing a wet kiss, full on Phil's lips.

"Wait a second. I didn't say I would have one. I only said you make it hard to say no," Phil answered.

"Well. Whatever. Have it your own way. I still have to get some ice for my drink!" she retorted, her voice rising in anger.

Phil sat alone in the room thinking. He knew that if he continued to stay with Ki, she would continue to insist he drink with her. What he didn't know was, to what extent she would go, to convince him. But he did know that, if the means by she had already resorted to was an indication, he was hopelessly lost and would surrender to temptation.

His mind raced, reminding him he was a "man," and that he was "only human". Suddenly, the realization came; he knew he must leave.

He didn't hesitate. Quickly getting up, he quietly walked to the door and let himself out. He didn't exactly remember his way, but he started in a direction he believed to be the way downstairs. Reaching the end of the hallway, he was relieved to find himself on the landing to the stairway.

Descending the stairs, he paused at street level and realized the stairs he had just used were not the same one they had used, less than two hours ago. He momentarily stopped, trying to orient himself, and get a sense of direction. It was very difficult in the darkness because all of the buildings looked exactly the same. He wandered aimlessly around for about a half hour, until he finally recognized a street he remembered. He turned in the direction he believed would lead him to the waterfront and to the ship.

At 4:15 AM he spotted the troop ship lying in the harbor, and doggedly headed for it thinking how good it was going to feel To "sack out." His only regret was having to leave Harve in his drunken state. Remembering the difficulty he had finding his way back to the ship, he knew Harve would get completely lost.

In the cold gray dawn, a resounding crash awakened Phil. He bolted upright to a sitting position in his bunk. In so doing, he hit his head on the bunk above. He bit his lip to keep from crying out in pain. Glancing at the luminous hands of his watch he noted it was 07:30 Hours. He had been asleep less than 3 hours. He noted the bunk above, which had been empty when he sacked out, now sagged, with the weight of another soldier. He then realized the loud crash, disrupting his sleep, had been caused by his friend, Harve, returning to the ship, tripping over something in the darkness. Phil was amused, and relieved, when the sound of snoring reached his ears. Harve had found his way back to the ship.

Formations and military protocol had been relaxed onboard the U.S. Army Troop Ship, since all soldiers had been accounted for at onboarding, embankment from home port.

The only fixed schedule was for chow times. Breakfast at 07:00 Hours; Lunch at 12:00 Hours, and Dinner at 05:00 Hours.

The sun had already started to rise when Phil groggily climbed from his bunk, showered, shaved, dressed and started to head for the galley for breakfast when he remembered Harve was still sleeping. Doing an about face, he headed back to the sleeping quarters to wake him up. He approached Havre's bunk, grabbed him by the shoulder, and shook him awake.

"Huh? Huh? Uhhh… what?" Harve responded, and buried his head deeper in the covers.

"Come on, Harve, you better get up, if you want anything to eat before the galley closes.

"No! Go away! Don't bother me!" Harve demanded in a garbled voice.

"Come on, Harve. Wake up! Wake up, Man!" Phil said, grabbing his shoulder, and vigorously shaking him.

Harve sat bolt upright on the bunk and stormily demanded, "What the hell's the idea of waking me up in the middle of the night?"

"It's not the middle of the night. It's the middle of the morning, to be exact," Phil shot back.

Harve shook his head, to clear away the sleep of hangover, looked daggers at Phil and shouted a question at him, "Why the hell did you run out on me last night. You dirty little bastard!"

"I didn't run out on you, Harve. I just didn't like the company I was with," Phil softly replied remembering a Bible verse he had heard, that said, 'A soft voice turns away wrath,' (Proverbs 15:1). Besides, you were doing alright. Why should it matter to you that I disappeared?"

"You know where I woke up this morning?"

"No. Where did you wake up?" Phil asked genuinely concerned.

"I woke up in an alley this morning, with my pockets turned inside out, and my wallet stripped," Harve explained.

"How did that happen?" Phil questioned.

"After I left Mia's place I was drunk as hell. I got lost and couldn't even find a rickshaw driver to bring me back to the ship. Staggering around, I got mugged and knocked unconscious. I was woken up by two MP's (Military Police) who gave me a ride to the ship.

"I'm really sorry to hear that, Harve. It's good you did not end up in jail, or the hospital," Phil consoled him.

"Aw. Hell. Don't feel sorry for me. It was my own damn fault. I broke a promised to myself that I would never get falling down drunk again. But to think, I broke that promise to myself, all for a lotta drinks, and a little 'nooky' (sex)."

"I got out of there when I could; I passed on the "nooky," Phil replied.

"Yeah! Wish I had of. I wish I had your will power," Harve complimented Phil.

"Well. If you hang out with me long enough, maybe you will," Phil assured him.

"Yeah. Maybe. Don't count on it. Only God knows," Harve replied.

By the time Harve had showered, shaved, and dressed, his anger at Phil had dampened, and they were ready for breakfast.

As he and Harve stepped out onto the deck Phil breathed deeply of the fresh, salt air. He was still sleepy even though he had managed to get about seven hours of sleep. His growling stomach reminded him he had not eaten in many hours. Even the thought of food made him hungrier.

Over breakfast Phil could not control his laughter about Harve's telling his story of being mugged and having his wallet robbed of his money.

Phil attempted to stifle his laughter. Harve asked "What's so funny?"

"I'm sorry, Harve, I can't help but laugh about your situation of getting mugged. I know to you, it's not funny, but it could have been a lot worse. That's the reward for sinful living. No offense," Phil said, extending his hand.

"I accept your apology, Phil but don't go spouting off any of that Holy Joe Scripture jazz at me."

"I wasn't planning on it, Harve. I know, that you know, the circumstances which happened to you, would not have happened if you had not started drinking.

"Let me just share one verse of Scripture, and I promise, I will not quote any more today. The Bible says, 'Whatever a man sows, that shall he also reap.' (Galatians 6:7). That's my Scripture for you today. Now let's enjoy our breakfast," Phil said with a smile.

"I don't feel like eating very much, but I can sure go for some coffee," Harve replied.

After breakfast, leaving the galley, they both were absorbed in their own thoughts.

CHAPTER 20

Eternity

At 08:00 Hours the following day, the military address system pierced the stillness of the morning, and quieted the boisterous chatter of the troops.

"Now hear this! Now hear this! To all Infantry personnel on this U.S. Army Transport Ship, by direction of the Commanding Officer, you are ordered to immediately assemble on deck!"

For just over a week, the Transport Ship had been at anchor in the harbor waiting orders to deliver the troops to combat duty.

Troops hurriedly responded to the order for assembly knowing "this was it".

In less than five minutes, the troops assembled in rank formation on deck standing at attention, awaiting the arrival of the Commanding General.

The General appeared on the Captain's Bridge, and surveyed the troops for a full thirty seconds before speaking. "At Ease!" the Commander ordered. "We have just received our orders. Briefly, we are to proceed to Pusan and assist in holding the beachhead that has just been established. We will be receiving reinforcements from the US Army Allied Nation Military shortly after arriving to secure the Pusan beachhead. We will be pulling out of here at 18:30 Hours, to meet and transfer all personnel to an LST (Landing Ship for Tanks, Troops, and Equipment) and arrive under cover of darkness."

"May I suggest, you catch up on writing those overdue letters home? For security reasons, be careful what you write. All personnel are restricted to quarters. That will be all. Commanders, dismiss your companies!" boomed the voice of the Commanding General.

"Company; Ten Hut; Dismissed!" came the commander's order.

At the word "dismissed," almost with one voice, a loud shout of "*'HuuuuAaaaah!*" went up from the troops, expressing understanding, that at last they were going to *use* what they had been taught to do, and *why* they had been sent over to use it. The challenge of fighting the enemy; to kill, or be killed.

With an air of excitement, Phil and Harve walked toward their quarters discussing the recent order to duty.

"Well Harve, this is what we have been waiting for," Phil said.

"Aw hell. There won't be much fightin' on Pusan. It's already been established. All we'll be doin' is helpin' to hold it," Harve replied, in disappointment.

"You sound disappointed, Are you?" Phil asked.

"Sure! The establishing troops will receive all the credit! We will just be baby sittin' errand boys!" he replied in a disgusted voice.

"You are never satisfied, are you, Harve? You always find something to complain about. As a matter of fact. If someone gave you a million dollars you would complain because you had to pay income tax on it," Phil replied in a less critical voice than what he had started with.

Pusan was much like Harve had predicted, with occasional sounds of war, but for the most part, relatively quiet. His unit was ordered to just maintain securing of the beachhead, and to do a general "mopping up" exercise.

By the time reinforcement troops arrived, organized resistance seemed to have disappeared with North Korean Communist troops retreating back toward Manchuria.

Troops were exceeding happy when the U.S Army Commanding General pronounced a Peace Accord had been reached, and that the war was over except for a mopping up exercise.

The United Nations General Assembly recommended that appropriate steps be taken to assure conditions of stability occurred throughout both South and North Korea.

Under this loose edict American forces advanced northward toward the Manchurian border in a movement to unite all of Korea. There was little reason to believe Communist Red China would enter the war.

Then the unexpected happened. Bearing arms captured from Chinese Nationalists, Communist Red China forces swarmed across the border into Korea. Although posing as "Volunteers" they really were in the Chinese Communist Army which was heavily supported by war planes commanded and manned by Communist Russia. From all outward appearances it was another undeclared war.

American forces overpowered by the onslaught were forced to retreat toward the 38th. Parallel as fast as they had recently advanced toward and beyond it.

Infantry Units, including Phil and Harve's, were reassigned away from defending the Pusan beachhead and were drawn into heavy combat battle.

The mud and muck ran knee deep and the weather was bitterly cold. The hills of Korea were slick and slimy, as the monsoon rains fell. The putrid smell of dead Japanese soldier bodies filled the air.

Coming off guard duty, Phil wondered how long they had been fighting. He climbed into the foxhole next to Harve, who was already dozing. He huddled close to Harve, who was now the Squad leader he had been assigned to, trying to absorb some heat from Havre's body. Shaking from the cold, he watched the mud ooze in over the top of his boots. Trying to answer his own question he was trying to think; had it been four, five, or six days? They had been on the MLR (Main line of Resistances). "Oh, well. What difference does it make?" he asked himself. Too tired to think, he leaned his head against the damp side of the foxhole and closed his eyes, taking advantage of the lull in fighting.

The pattern of defense, set by both the Korean and Russian Communist forces, ever since they had launched their surprise counter attack, had been to blast away with artillery fire, and then the chatter of 50 caliber machine gun fire shattered the night.

Red, fiery, streams of tracer bullets being fired, split the blackness and echoed the sound of battle and then the night would be heavy with silence.

The next thing Phil and Harve knew, they were being alerted by a guard sentinel, saying in a low, heavy gruff voice, "Hey, you guys. Heads up. I think we are being surrounded, and closed in on, by 'gooks,' (a slang name for Japanese soldiers), I been seein' a lot of movement out there," the guard said, gesturing toward the MLR (Main Line of Resistance).

Quickly coming up from the bottom of the foxhole Phil and Harve grabbed their M-1 rifles and stared off into the darkness surrounding them.

Harve said to the guard, "OK, thanks, Rice. Give a heads-up warning to the rest to my squad."

The sentinel moved on to another foxhole, to warn others.

"Do you see anything, Phil?" Harve asked in a hushed voice.

"No. I can't see a thing," Phil replied in a whisper.

"I think Rice was seein' things, or else he found a bottle somewhere. I wish he had let me doze. I was havin' a real good dream, and now, I'll never know, how I made out with that chick," he said with a grin.

"You pick a fine time to dream about women," Phil chided him.

"Well. I can't think of anything better to dream about. What time is it?" he commented, and asked.

Looking at the luminous hands of his watch Phil replied, "It's 0430 hours. It'll be daylight in another hour."

He wouldn't be wrong from his estimate. The sky was already getting lighter in the east, and the terrain was beginning to take shape in the gray dawn hour.

Suddenly, without warning, there was the swish of an artillery round projectile landing and exploding behind them. Immediately, the sky itself seemed to explode with air bursts from artillery fire.

"They're using illuminating phosphorus fire," Phil yelled above the noise of explosions.

"And here they come!" Harve yelled in response, pointing in the enemy direction.

Phil followed the line of direction Harve was pointing, and saw hundreds of enemy figures on the horizon looming over the slope, approximately a thousand yards to their left flank. Then the figures disappeared, merging with the contour of the land.

"Now you see 'em; now you don't, Harve said, leaning against the side of the foxhole, with only his rifle and head exposed.

"Wish they'd show themselves long enough for me to get a bead on 'em. I'd blow 'em to kingdom come."

"You may get the chance. Look!" Phil said.

"What?" Harve asked.

"There. Coming through the brush," Phil replied pointing.

"The dirty, bastard gooks, trying to keep us under cover with illuminating phosphorus fire, so they can sneak up on us," Harve grumbled.

They stopped talking and remained motionless. They observed a hunched-over figure zigzagging his way through the clumps of brush less than a hundred yards away. Phil felt a chill run up his spine, and his hands grew clammy on the cold steel of his rifle. Sweat ran down his face as the sniper moved in on them. Phil raised his rifle sighting down the barrel. Twenty-five yards… fifteen…, the figure was a perfect target. His mind race with questions, "Why do I have to kill him? I don't even know him. I'm not mad at him," his finger closed on the trigger…the sniper stopped in his tracks. He appeared to be looking directly into Phil's face as the impact of the bullet caused his knees to give way under him and he slowly slumped forward.

Phil shuddered and breathed a prayer of forgiveness, "Oh, God forgive me."

"You got 'em; Just like shooting ducks in a pond!" Harve yelled with glee.

This was only the beginning. They looked out across the field to see masses of so called "gooks" advancing toward them. Realizing they had given away their position by the flash of gunfire killing the advance sniper, they hunkering down in the foxhole, and bravely stood their ground, hoping friendly fire would save them, as they watched Japanese soldiers going down, under the American aircraft strafing the battleground.

Again, the communist army had switched tactics, and were now at the expense of their own combat troops, firing in among their own ground forces with artillery fire in an attempt to drive the American troops back... back... back...

It was a long, tiring, and disagreeable time for the American forces as they continued to fight and maintain a defense in the face of counter-attacks by the Communist Chinese and Russian armies. The battle had been hot and heavy as a result of the Communist's on-slaught, because the enemy had, to coin a phrase, "thrown everything they had except the kitchen sink" at them, causing many wounded and fatalities to the American, and Allied Nation Armies.

The early evening dusk blackened into darkness, and then there was silence, as the heat of the battle subsided.

Due to the rapid movement of Communist Chinese and Russian troops, the American forces had been forced to momentarily retreat.

Phil had become separated from his Unit, and Squad Leader Harve. Neither knew where the other was, or how far back they had retreated. They did not know, if they were in enemy territory, or surrounded by their own troops.

Having reunited, and secured themselves in a newly dug foxhole Phil and Harve begin to relax in the shelter of the foxhole.

The lull of battle continued, and the silence became oppressive, almost deafening, after the raucous, deafening sound of artillery fire, machine gun chatter, and mortar explosions.

Consistent with human nature when imminent danger withdraws its fangs, man becomes careless. Harve was no exception. Pulling a rumpled pack of cigarettes from his jacket, he squatted down in the foxhole and lighted a match. The bright flame of the match illuminated the dark of the night, and outlined the silhouette of the foxhole. Phil who had remained standing, straining his eyes to see into the darkness, dropped to his knees, and turning to Harve demanded in a hushed voice, "Put out that light!"

Harve was surprised at the intense anger in Phil's voice.

In an embarrassed voice, realizing the foolishness of what he had done said, "Well… I was only trying to light a smoke."

"You're only trying to get us killed. Do you know the light from a match can be seen for two miles at night?" Phil demanded.

"We'll never get out of this alive anyway. What's the difference whether we get it now or later? Besides, you told me you weren't afraid to die. What's the matter? Have you changed your mind?" Harve questioned Phil with a note of sarcasm.

"Yes. I did tell you that, Harve, and I meant it. I'm not afraid to die because I know where I will go. But I'm afraid for you to die. Do you know where your soul will go, if you died this very moment?" Phil asked.

"Sure. I would go into a grave, six feet under, pushin' up daisies." Harve flippantly replied.

"I had forgotten you once told me you didn't believe in Heaven or Hell. I didn't believe you then, and I still don't. It is the in-born nature of man to believe in some form of Higher Power. You're no different from anyone else. You display this attitude. You say that because you don't understand the things that relate to God, and the things of God. But really, you are trying to justify your reason for living the life you live," Phil continued.

"Oh, I guess there is a God. But I have never taken the time to explore the possibility. Besides, there is too much, I don't understand," Harve explained.

"Harve, it really doesn't matter if you don't understand, because the Bible says, 'It is by faith, through grace you are saved' (Ephesians 2:8). So, it isn't necessary for you to understand these providential things, but it is necessary for you to have faith to accept them. Because the Bible also says, 'Without faith it is impossible to please God.'" (Hebrews 11:6).

Phil asked, "Tell me, Harve, if a man was hungry, and he sat down to a table filled with food, but he refused to eat, until he heard a scientific solution for the process of germination, fermentation, and digestion, what would you think of him? A fool? Sure, you would. If, on the other hand, your soul is hungry, don't quibble about the things you don't understand, take of the Bread of Life', then you'll begin to understand." Phil explained.

"You may be right, Phil. I don't suppose I'll ever live to find out," Harve stubbornly replied.

Phil said, "Yes, Harve, one day you'll die, and you'll find out I was right, if you don't do something about your salvation."

Phil continued witnessing, "Why don't you get down on your knees, right here in this foxhole, admit to God you are a sinner, say you repent of your sin, ask forgiveness for your sin, and invite Jesus Christ to become your Personal Savior today?" Phil's continued, his voice compelling, and his heart heavy, under the burden of sin that shackled his friend.

"Uhhh…let me think about what you've said, and then I'll make up my mind," Harve hedged on giving a direct answer.

"Ok, Harve. I don't want you to think I have been preaching to you. But I want to impress upon you the importance of being ready to die, especially under these war time circumstances.

"Before we change the subject, I don't want to leave you with the impression that I'm afraid to die. I want you to know that, as much as I would like to go on living, I would gladly lay down my life to see you turn your life around, from your unbelieving, sinful life, to a saving belief in God," Phil finished his testimony to Harve.

The piercing scream of a mortar projectile shattered the stillness landed and exploded within the perimeter of the foxhole that had been silhouetted, when Harve lit the match. Then all hell broke loose. The enemy resumed the battle with a vigorous attack, on the American forces. For their safety, Harve and Phil dived to the bottom of the foxhole. Harve buried his face in the mud with his body in a half prone position.

Phil fell across Harve because the bottom of the foxhole would not accommodate both of them. They had no sooner hit the bottom of the foxhole when a blinding flash, and resounding explosion shook the earth around them.

As the sound of the explosion died away fragments of steel shrapnel could be heard dropping close to them. For several minutes after the explosion the two men lay on the bottom of the foxhole. Harve bore the major part of Phil's weight in that position and said to Phil, "Hey, Man. It would be alright if you get up now. You're breakin' my back."

Receiving no response from Phil, Harve again said, "Aw right, Man. This is no time to be laying down on the job. Please get off my back."

Still not receiving a response from Phil, Harve, sensing something was wrong, wiggled and squirmed his way out from under the weight of Phil's body and struggled to a sitting position.

Phil's prostate form slumped back down to the bottom of the foxhole. Harve tried to revive Phil by cradling him in his arms, and forcing him to drink some water out of his canteen.

Harve was convinced the repercussion from the blast had knocked Phil unconscious, until he felt a wet, warm, and sticky liquid seeping through Phil's field jacket, and spreading down the front.

Harve almost panicked. Instead, he turned the canteen upside down letting the water pour over Phil's face, at the same time calling out, "Phil! Phil! Can you hear me?" almost screaming the words. When there was still no answer, Harve placed his ear close to Phil's mouth to see if he was breathing.

About the same time, he felt Phil move in his arms. Harve frantically shook Phil and spoke to him. "Phil! Phil! Answer me! Do you hear me?"

Phil stirred and begin to speak in a labored voice. "Yes…I…hear you…you…Harve."

Harve said, "Don't try to talk, Man. Save your strength. I'll get help".

"No…it's no use…I'm beyond help…God's cal…cal ling me ho…me…Tell… my…fam…fa…family I lov…love th…them," Phil said, breathing heavily.

"No! You're gonna' be alright! You're gonna' be alright!" Harve said trying to convince himself, more than Phil. And called out, "Medic! Medic! Help Medic!

"It's…no…use they…will never…hear you," Phil said, his voice growing weaker.

"Yes! Yes! They will hear me. I'll make them hear me!" Harve said, as he continued to frantically call out at, the top of his lungs, "Medic! Medic! Over here! Medic! Help Medic!"

Phil feebly reached up grabbing Harve by the neck and pulled him down so he could speak into his ear, "Har…Harve…I said…I wou… would glad…gladly…give my life…to see…yo…you…acc…accept Chris…Christ…as you… your…Per…Personal Sav… Sav… Savior. I di…didn't …know it…wou…would come…to this…but I'll se…see you…in He…Heaven." Phil's body gave a convulsive jerk, and his head dropped limply back over Harve's arm.

Turning tear dimmed eyes toward Heaven, Harve remorsefully exclaimed, "Oh, My God! Oh, My God! What have I done? "What have I done?" God, can you forgive me? Will you forgive me? And save my soul?" Like Phil said, "Will you become my Personal Savior?"

www.ingramcontent.com/pod-product-compliance
Lightning Source LLC
Chambersburg PA
CBHW031019190726
48286CB00003BA/924